THE AGE OF CHAOS
THE MULTIVERSE OF MICHAEL MOORCOCK

THE AGE OF CHAOS
THE MULTIVERSE OF MICHAEL MOORCOCK

JEFF GARDINER

First published in Great Britain in 2002 by

The British Fantasy Society
201 Reddish Road, South Reddish,
Stockport, SK5 7HR

**Publication edited and co-ordinated by David J Howe
for the British Fantasy Society.**

With grateful thanks to Rosemary Howe and Mike Chinn for proof reading.
Thanks also to Michael Moorcock and Andy Cox.

Jeff Gardiner can be contacted at JAGardiner@aol.com

ISBN 0 9538681 1 7 (paperback)
ISBN 0 9538681 2 5 (hardback)
BFS 008

British Library Cataloguing in Publication Data.
A catalogue record for this book is available from the British Library.

Printed in England by Publish on Demand Ltd,
Aberdeen Studios, 22-24 Highbury Grove,
London, N5 2EA

3 4 5 6 7 8 9 10 11 12 13 14 15

CONTENTS

Thanks to my wife, Sandy,
for all her support and patience.

Introduction
By Michael Moorcock

How do you judge a book which is about yourself? Naturally, if it is kind, you are flattered. Then you are concerned that it doesn't somehow misrepresent you and that it has its facts right, and then you read it to see if it offers you any fresh ideas on your own stuff. Jeff Gardiner's excellent book has offered me many fresh insights into my own work and it will remain, for me at least, a very useful reference when I have one of those increasingly frequent moments of not knowing what's going on in my own fiction, let alone my life. I don't have a habit of rereading my own work and so much of Jeff Gardiner's detailed study is pretty fresh to me. I feel, therefore, that I can recommend it as a pretty useful guide to the variety of fiction I've turned out over what in 2005 will be a fifty year career as a professional writer. Whether it is of any use to other writers, they will know best, but I think it should help the casual reader to get a better grip on the vast raft of stuff I've produced and also, I hope, give them an idea about what they would like to read and what doesn't interest them.

I must admit I pity any reader coming to my work for the first time and wondering where on earth they should begin. It tends to baffle me, let alone them. And when I am asked to recommend something of my own, I find it very hard to do. Readers who love *Mother London*, for instance, might not care for *The Sundered Worlds* at all and Hawkmoon fans might be bored to the teeth with *King of the City*. My father's personal favourite of mine was *Kane Of Old Mars*, which was closest to the Edgar Rice Burroughs romances I first started reading in his copies. I have an old-fashioned idea about my profession. I believe I should be able to turn my hand to almost any form at the drop of a hat – *belles-lettres*, criticism, fiction of various kinds, film scripts, tv work, short stories, novels, reminiscence, music and lyrics, whatever you can do. I think that some ideas are best expressed in semi-fiction, some in fiction, some in non-fiction and so on. Genres present their own methods. You use the best tools for the job. Some ideas are more suitable for essays, some for fiction. I also have ideas for novels which suit certain methods or express certain ideas best. I have written spoof detective stories, westerns and fantasy stories. I have written mostly non-modernist literary fiction but on occasions I have used modernist techniques because they are best suited to what I have to say. I have a habit of putting some of my most thoughtful notions into comic books. Until recently, my best description of 'the multiverse' was in the DC graphic novel, *Michael Moorcock's Multiverse*, which a number of my readers found impossible to understand. There is a way of reading a modern graphic novel which, to some degree, you have to learn, just as children have to learn the sequence of an ordinary sentence. Equally, there is a specialist vocabulary in fantasy and science fiction circles which often baffles the casual reader and indeed can act to alienate them from work they might otherwise enjoy. For this reason, I tend to start every fantasy book I write as if neither I nor my reader had read a fantasy novel before. I believe this helps to keep the book's vitality and interest, as well as being generally more user friendly! This method tends to give me, as far as I can tell, a slightly broader general audience than the average genre writer while making me slightly marginal to the genre audience, who are sometimes suspicious of what they might see as my divided loyalties!

Whatever my qualities as a writer, I am hard to pigeonhole. Critics who see me as 'sampling' different genres don't quite understand that I am not much interested in the genres themselves, just what the genres can offer me. While I've written Kit Carson and Buffalo Bill stories for juvenile weeklies, my adult ventures into their galloping grounds have been satirical or making some specific use of the local mythology. I actually have very little nostalgia for adventure fiction and my own leisure reading tends to be the likes of Elizabeth Bowen, Elizabeth Taylor and Angus Wilson. I can get very enthusiastic about *Death of the Heart* but remembered a short while ago that I never actually finished *Lord of the Rings*. I still don't know how it ends. This means that I have very few adult enthusiasms within the fantasy and sf genres, though I do greatly admire individual writers like M. John Harrison who write their own highly idiosyncratic fiction and who are as hard to pigeonhole as I am. I know that I'm a bit of an academic's nightmare. Add to my various literary enthusiasms, my musical career and my career as an editor of a fairly wide variety of publications, and it's no surprise to me to hear that some researchers and writers have actually lost their sanity before they could finish their bibliographies of my stuff, let alone begun their theses. Sometimes just finding the more obscure bits and pieces themselves is daunting and I am of no use, being bad at dates and record-keeping in general. For that reason, if no other, I can genuinely celebrate the publication of this book. It lifts some of my own confusion and I'm pretty sure it will lift some of yours. I welcome its publication especially since its author still manages to retain a convincing veneer of sanity and is, by all accounts, recovering well.

Michael Moorcock,
Circle Squared Ranch,
Lost Pines,
Texas, USA,
January 2002.

Prelude

Fantasy writer Angela Carter called Michael Moorcock "the master story-teller of our time" – a well-deserved title for an author who has influenced the literary world for over forty years. Carter, herself an avid reader of Moorcock, was keen to celebrate the importance of his work. In her enthusiastic review of *Mother London* in the *Guardian*, she concludes that: "Posterity will certainly give him that due place in the English literature of the late twentieth century which his more anaemic contemporaries grudge; indeed, he is so prolific it will probably look as though he has written most of it anyway."

Michael Moorcock is one of Britain's greatest writers and he is possibly the most consistently experimental author in the world of fantasy literature. Not only did he practically invent modern British fantasy and reshape science fiction as an editor, but he is also an exponent of mainstream literature. Whilst he rejects the notion of being a genre writer, much of his later fiction could be described as fantastic realism, although he is probably most famous for his fantasy hero Elric the albino and for that icon of 1960s psychedelia, Jerry Cornelius. In *The Encyclopedia of Fantasy*, the 'bible' for all fantasy fans, John Clute calls Moorcock, "the most important UK fantasy author of the 1960s and 1970s." This is misleading, as he continues to write prolifically into the 21st century and it could be argued that his later novels are amongst his best work. Clute does, however, suggest that Moorcock is "altogether the most significant UK author of sword and sorcery" and it is probably for his Eternal Champion novels that he will be most widely remembered. The extent of Moorcock's popularity is demonstrated by his world-wide following, led by an active international appreciation society, The Nomads of the Time Streams, and by the fact that his work is translated into many languages. Type his name into any internet search engine and you will encounter innumerable websites that pay homage to him. What is most impressive about Michael Moorcock is that he continues to produce novels, stories and non-fiction to such a high standard.

Michael Moorcock has won two World Fantasy Awards, including one in 2000 for Lifetime Achievement; a Nebula award; The *Guardian* Fiction Prize; a John W. Campbell Memorial Award and even a nomination for the Whitbread Prize. He also has a collection of six British Fantasy Awards: four August Derleth Awards, one for the short story category and in 1992 he won the British Fantasy Society's Special Award for his lifetime achievement. Moorcock has about a hundred books to his name, some of which are republished and retitled editions of earlier works, and this can prove bewildering to the uninitiated. My own Moorcock bibliography can be found in the Appendix at the back of this book.

Moorcock has written about fantasy forms in literature in his book, *Wizardry and Wild Romance,* one of the best books about fantasy by a fantasist, and he both acknowledges and proves through his own writing that fantasy is an important and often under-valued art form. Fantasy creates a tension between what is real and unreal, and this echoes Moorcock's balance between order and chaos. Whilst Moorcock acknowledges the part that fantasy has played in his own success he does admit: "I have difficulty defining 'Fantasy' as a readily definable genre – or frequently even as an element. I don't believe that any technique or method is more or less useful than another – everything depends upon individual human talent in the end."

His dislike for generic terms is expressed in the following way: "I don't believe there is such a thing as fantasy or science fiction or detective fiction and so on. I think there are certain writers who in their field shine and in every one of those fields you'll get some good writers emerging. Sometimes the field itself can limit the writer's work and then frequently the writer does something about it."

Moorcock is a protean writer, whose work transcends literary and generic boundaries: like Charles Dickens, his novels are, paradoxically, both popular and literary. His writing covers fields as far ranging as romance, heroic fantasy, science fiction, fabulation, surrealism, popular fiction, satire, allegory, fantastic realism, post-modernism, non-fiction, rock'n'roll, comics and even cinema. His novels defy categorisation because they are greater than the limitations of the critic's vocabulary. As a 'literary' writer Moorcock shows artistic ability in his myth-making and story-telling; his creation of intriguing characters; the subtle irony and ornate vocabulary; an exploitation of metaphor and allegory; and his presentation of imaginary landscapes and emotional relationships. However, his greatest desire is to be a popular author.

He first came to prominence in 1964 as the editor of *New Worlds* magazine with his radical editorial approach that alienated many science fiction fans, but also won him great respect as a writer of vision whose vocabulary and ideas were second to none. His own early stories best exemplify his desire to experiment with structures, themes and language. It was in these early stories that he began to develop the symbolism and subjects that continue to dominate his later writings.

Michael Moorcock is incredibly prolific and what causes the most confusion is the interlinking nature of all his novels. Most of his books fit into a particular mythos or are related to a series of novels, although which one or how is not always immediately obvious. Beginning with a brief autobiographical sketch, this book examines Moorcock's early career as an editor for the avant-garde literary magazine *New Worlds*, and then evaluates his early fantasy and the famous world of Jerry Cornelius that arose from the magazine. Then each chapter discusses a major work or series and attempts to do so in chronological order; that is by the date of the first book in each series. Any confusion might be caused by the fact that Moorcock does not write his books in any seemingly logical order, and so many of his novels and short stories are repackaged and reprinted.

In this book you will find biographical detail, because to appreciate Moorcock's work means understanding the writer. Moorcock's influence on speculative fiction is evaluated and the Eternal Champion – Elric, Corum, Hawkmoon, Ereköse and Von Bek – is assessed. Also examined are Jerry Cornelius, the spoof messiah of swinging London; the comic fantasy of *The Dancers at the End of Time; Gloriana*; the crazed memoirs of Colonel Pyat; the fantastic realism of *Mother London* and its sequel, *King of the City;* and finally some of Moorcock's later works.

The purpose of this book is to celebrate the achievements of one of fantasy's leading figures. Fans should find this book a useful tool to explore the multiverse even further and those who are new to Moorcock's work might catch a glimpse of the inspiration behind his mercurial mind. Moorcock successfully creates memorable characters and mystical landscapes using irrepressible wit and exotic language reminding us all just how fantasy continues to be one of literature's sharpest tools, as well as the key to developing the imagination.

1: THE MASTER STORY-TELLER

Born in Mitcham, South London in 1939, Michael Moorcock was a child of the war. He remembers exploring bombed buildings, collecting shrapnel, playing in air-raid shelters, watching barrage balloons, dog-fights in the sky, and the destruction of the blitz. These vivid memories deeply influenced his imagination and the ruined landscapes would be used later in his descriptions of war-torn cities in his heroic fantasies, as well as in *Mother London*. Moorcock admits that his "futuristic landscapes are symbolic portrayals of the London blitz." He was disappointed when the war ended, which meant the end of great adventure and excitement, and stories of glory and heroism.

His father left home when he was six and the young Michael was sent away to school. A couple of formative years were spent at the Michael Hall Steiner Waldorf School in Forest Row, Sussex. Steiner schools emphasise the spiritual, physiological and artistic aspects of education and prefer to think of learning as a mystical journey for each pupil who is very much an individual. Moorcock states that "my school did actually shape my life" and the Steiner philosophy not only encouraged his wild imagination but also inspired many of his ideas for the 'multiverse', which he was later to develop through his writing. It is likely that Steiner's "cosmic Christianity", as Moorcock calls it, also influenced his political allegiance to anarchism. The young Michael was expelled for his attempted escapes and story-telling, which were a result of his youthful exuberance and over-active imagination. He was reading classics and popular literature from an early age and would entertain his dormitory at night with fantastic tales. He professes having an early love for Charles Dickens, Edith Nesbitt, E R Burroughs and H Rider Haggard, amongst others. Later influences included Mervyn Peake, George Meredith and Fritz Leiber. Moorcock claims to have read George Bernard Shaw at the age of five.

Whilst at school he was already typing his own 'fanzines', the first being 'Outlaw's Own' in 1949, written at the age of nine, followed by several others including 'Book Collector's News' and eighteen issues of 'Burroughsania' on Edgar Rice Burroughs and related authors. Before he left school aged fifteen he was already a serious book collector with useful contacts in publishing and bookselling, and had written his first novel – a self-indulgent piece of adolescent juvenilia about life in Soho, which was never sent to a publisher but got left for years during which it was stored in a Ladbroke Grove basement where it was eaten by rats. To this day he is still a serious book and magazine collector.

His first jobs were all in London and included being a messenger for a shipping company and then an office boy for a firm of management consultants, a job that allowed him to continue printing fanzines using the company equipment. At sixteen he was asked to write a heroic fantasy story for a comic magazine and his Sojan stories, which owe something to Edgar Rice Burroughs and Robert Howard's Conan, were accepted. At the age of seventeen he became the full-time editor of *Tarzan Adventures* on a wage of six pounds a week, and was writing comic strips for 'Kit Carson', 'Billy the Kid', and other heroes of 'Lion' and 'Tiger' Annuals. By the time he was twenty, Moorcock had joined the Sexton Blake Library as editor, and at least one book, *Caribbean Crisis*, was written fully by him, but rewritten in house and attributed to the house pseudonym, Desmond Reid. The political emphasis was completely reversed. This much sought after novella is available to read on the internet and is a typical Sexton Blake mystery in which the indomitable hero prevents a communist revolution on a Caribbean island. Moorcock's first story published under his own name was a collaboration with author

Barrington Bayley called 'Peace on Earth', printed in *New Worlds* magazine in 1959. The next breakthrough occurred when the editor of *New Worlds*, Ted Carnell, commissioned from Moorcock a fantasy series for a sister magazine, *Science Fantasy*. This was to be the series that introduced Elric the albino prince, arguably Moorcock's most popular and enduring character. Carnell also commissioned 'Aspects of Fantasy' a series of informative polemics which would later form the basis of *Wizardry and Wild Romance*. Moorcock states that 'My fantasy stories were to a degree an attempt to demonstrate points I was making in the articles'.

Still in his early twenties Moorcock left his employers to become a full-time writer and journalist, then for a while worked as a staff editor and writer for the Liberal Party. He also travelled widely, drank extensively and even claims to have had visions when he was ill, seeing images of Christ or buildings shimmering, which he insists were not aided by hallucinogenics. Moorcock's lifestyle could be described as bohemian and he had long admired the liberal aestheticism of John Ruskin and the pale epicurianism of the fin-de-siècle. Moorcock's lifestyle at this time is best described as one of sensuality and excess.

He was an obsessive writer; sometimes writing a hundred pages a day if necessary, although he found scripting comic strips more financially rewarding than novel writing. He realised that he could earn as much as fifty pounds a day, but unfortunately he also had the inclination and capacity to drink it all the next. He also experimented with drugs, but always insisted that drugs should be used responsibly and that they were useless as aids to writing.

In April 1963, Moorcock was asked to contribute a guest editorial to *New Worlds* and then in 1964 he was invited to succeed Carnell as full-time editor of *New Worlds*, which he continued to do until 1974 (Issues 142 – 207) and came back to intermittently. This important post allowed him to be critical of the existing literary establishment and to experiment with forms and styles in his own writing.

During this fertile period two notable experimental Moorcock novels came to prominence, *The Final Programme* (1968), the first Jerry Cornelius novel, which subsequently became a film (Goodtime Films, directed by Robert Fuest in 1973) and *Behold The Man* (1969), which had won the Nebula Award as a novella in 1966. Meanwhile he was also developing his Eternal Champion stories for the magazine *Science Fantasy*, of which the characters Erekosë and Elric were particularly popular. Most of these stories were adapted into novels giving Moorcock some financial security and finding a particularly profitable market in America. *New Worlds* was successful under his editorship and it achieved its aims of discovering new talent and establishing innovative writing, but its publication became an exhausting task for Moorcock who was paying for it from his own pocket and it drained him both emotionally and physically. Their distributors went bankrupt and even a small Arts Council grant was not enough to run an ambitious magazine, so Moorcock published Brian Aldiss' novel *Report On Probability A* in 1967 because it had been turned down by Faber and Faber as they considered it to be too risky, to make extra money and the magazine changed format. The magazine nurtured what is now known as the 'New Wave' of speculative fiction; a 'movement' of sorts, which created such high feeling that sometimes led to fighting in the staff offices. Moorcock practically ran things single-handedly for ten years before he handed over the editorship, although he retained ownership of the title. Since the demise of the magazine in 1979, *New Worlds* has continued to exist as an occasional anthology of new short stories and from time to time publishes a special issue, such as a 50th anniversary edition.

Another source of income for Moorcock came from his music, and in the fifties and sixties there was a strong link between science fiction and rock'n'roll. Moorcock played guitar and banjo semi-professionally with skiffle band, The Greenhorns, and sang and played guitar for various other bands; enough to get a taste of the music scene as it began erupting in the early sixties with its bohemian lifestyle around Soho. He also travelled and played abroad, particularly in Paris. Then the 1970s saw Moorcock involved with London's Ladbroke Grove psychedelic scene, where such stars as David Bowie, Marc Bolan and Jimi Hendrix 'hung out'. He joined the cult band Hawkwind and rock music seemed to provide a fresh impetus for his writing.

Hawkwind are still seen by many as the champions of hippie space rock and having met Robert Calvert their lead singer through the underground magazine, *Frendz*, Moorcock performed with them at a number of concerts, frequently standing in for the unstable Calvert.

His contribution can be heard on several Hawkwind albums, including *Warrior on the Edge of Time* (1975) and *Live Chronicles* (1994), and he wrote lyrics for others, such as on *Choose Your Masques* (1980). His most recent contribution was in 2000, when he appeared 'electronically' with the band who performed live on stage. This concert is available on a CD called *Yule Ritual*. Their 1985 album, *The Chronicle of the Black Sword*, was based wholly on the Elric mythos. Hawkwind have a huge cult following and the band still play Moorcock songs, such as 'Sonic Attack', 'Kings of Speed' and 'Sleep of a Thousand Tears'.

Moorcock also wrote lyrics for heavy rock band Blue Oyster Cult and Moorcock's novel *The Fireclown* (aka *The Winds of Limbo*) inspired Pink Floyd's 'Set the Controls for the Heart of the Sun'. There are further rock music connections: Deep Purple named an album 'Stormbringer' after the Elric novel; Diamond Head paid homage to Elric on their 'Living On Borrowed Time' album; and the metal bands The Tygers of Pan Tang and Mourneblade took their names from Moorcock's books. Moorcock enjoys telling the anecdote of how he taught one friend to play his first three guitar chords and then that friend, called Peter Green, went on to co-found Fleetwood Mac.

Moorcock's own band, The Deep Fix, are named after one of his early stories and mentioned in the Jerry Cornelius novels as well as in *King of the City*. Moorcock and The Deep Fix cut the album *New World's Fair* in 1975, which was reissued on CD in 1995, and later released the cassette, *The Brothel in Rosenstrasse* (1992) to go with his novel of the same name. *The Entropy Tango* was planned as a novel and rock album tie-in, whilst *Gloriana* nearly became a musical. Moorcock even has his own entry in Tony Jasper's *The International Encyclopedia of Hard Rock and Heavy Metal*.

1978 saw the publication of *Gloriana* and since then Moorcock has written less heroic fantasy and shown more interest in fantastic realism, with the Colonel Pyat novels and the critically acclaimed *Mother London*. He has returned to the Elric mythos since, most notably in 1991 with *The Revenge of the Rose*, and followed in 2001 by *The Dreamthief's Daughter*, which begins the new Elric trilogy.

After two failed marriages, Moorcock met his third wife in America and has lived in Austin, Texas since 1994. The 1990s saw a revival in the UK of Moorcock's extensive canon with most of his novels and short stories enjoying revision and republication in omnibus form by Millennium/Orion who collected his back-list with the aim of linking much of his work to create a coherent and inter-linking series.

Moorcock has gone back to his own childhood heroes of pirates, highwaymen and the Wild West, particularly in *Tales from the Texas Woods* (1997), which includes a 'lost' Sherlock Holmes story. He even resurrects characters from his teenage years in comic strip writing: most notably Zenith the Albino and Sir Sexton Begg, a version of that famous London detective, Sexton Blake.

In interviews he often talks about his own talent for structuring novels and seeing the outline and forms before all else, and this is possibly his greatest strength. *Death Is No Obstacle*, a book of interviews with writer Colin Greenland, details his obsession with structure and Moorcock attempts to outline his sense of vision and style. He bases his structures on those constructions, moods and changes used by classical composers, such as Mozart, who Moorcock greatly admires.

The range of Moorcock's work is enormous, from Gothic romance to social commentary and it is easy to forget his extensive journalism, travel-writing and vociferous political support for anarchism and feminism. Moorcock also co-wrote the screenplay for the film, *The Land That Time Forgot*, and has been involved in developing an interactive computer game called *Silverheart,* based on the 2000 novel co-written with the popular British novelist Storm Constantine.

Moorcock has also embraced the internet as a place where he can communicate with his readers and he spends a great deal of time answering questions on a Question and Answer website. His answers are at times extensive and he has always been generous in the time he gives back to his fans and critics.

In his prolific career, Moorcock has always innovated and adhered to the principles he laid down in his editorial work for *New Worlds*, a magazine that may be his lasting legacy. In literary history, Moorcock is known as the editor who inspired the new wave of science fiction in the 1960s, and whilst this is true, it is important to remember that he has also achieved so much more through his own writing. His legacy is plain for anyone to see, particularly as he has inspired innumerable writers since, who have made public the debt they owe to Moorcock, most notably William Gibson, David Gemmell, Kim Newman, Neil Gaiman and Terry Pratchett. For his original fiction and his influence on modern literature, Moorcock deserves a more recognised place in British literary history.

2: Brave New Worlds

Although some of Moorcock's early novels used science fiction settings and imagery, his main impact in the sf field was as editor of *New Worlds* magazine, which became the flagship for the so-called 'New Wave of Science Fiction' in the 1960s and 70s. Moorcock, as an editor, certainly helped change the definitions of sf; his influence on the genre is an accepted part of sf history and the rise of the 'New Wave' became focused around the magazine, which attracted writers from Britain and America. Moorcock had had enough of formula sf with its sexist obsessions and preponderance of war against 'bug-eyed monsters' and he chose an sf magazine for his vision because that seemed the field most open to new ideas. Editor Ted Carnell, invited young writers to do guest editorials and Vol. 43, issue no.129 (April 1963) contained the now famous essay by a precocious Michael Moorcock, still in his early twenties, criticising science fiction in one of the leading sf magazines. Moorcock's main criticism was that most sf was unoriginal and lacked "passion, subtlety, irony, original characterisation, original and good style, a sense of involvement in human affairs, colour, density, depth and, on the whole, real feeling from the writer." Rather than "imitate slavishly what has gone on before" Moorcock called on new writers to exercise "passion and craftsmanship" in an attempt to create quality literature that blended fantasy and realism.

In his first editorial as editor of *New Worlds* (#142) Moorcock suggested that sf could be an acronym for 'speculative fantasy', and indeed the magazine began to break the rigid boundaries of science fiction, criticising 'golden age sf' in preference for the surreal fiction of, for example, William Burroughs. Moorcock had identified a "popular literary renaissance" and *New Worlds* was to be the vehicle. *New Worlds* contributor, and later, editor, Charles Platt explains in his book on sf and fantasy writers, *Dreammakers*, how Moorcock sustained much of the momentum: "he was iconoclastic and flamboyant. He became the editorial focus for new writing talent ... There was a sense of significance and destiny about the whole thing."

Moorcock had a vision for "a different kind of fiction ... (which) could come out of a marriage between experimental forms and old-style genre sf." Bored with the modernist novels of the fifties and sixties exemplified by Kingsley Amis, Moorcock became ambitious and with the help of J G Ballard began an experiment in form, narrative and language. *New Worlds* did more than revolutionise sf; it encouraged and nurtured a completely new direction in contemporary fiction. Moorcock was at pains to explain his use of terms, such as science fiction, much preferring 'science fantasy'. Many of the stories in *New Worlds* could be described as fantasy and rather than choose stories because they fitted a generic pattern, Moorcock selected anything original and inventively subversive, always keen to break down barriers and traditions.

Through his courageous editorial policy and his risky support of new talent, Moorcock single-handedly created this new form of speculative fiction, which became more concerned with man's alienation from the world, expressed through imagery rooted in the modern world and relevant to popular culture. As Moorcock wrote in one of his early editorials: "Through their fiction *New Worlds* writers are ... pioneers to the new, strange countries of the mind which will exist tomorrow. They have not lost their sense of wonder ... They are providing us with information, a language, a code, a new mythology ... as they continue the exploration of the interior."

The inspiration for this new mode of fiction came from pioneers as diverse as artist Salvador Dali whose paintings expressed a feeling of dilapidation and ennui; writer William Burroughs whose fragmented writing explored the inner mind and the human consciousness which has been heightened by drugs, leading to paranoia and other altered states; psychologist Carl Jung whose studies of myth and ritual were closely linked to imagination and spirituality; and rock hero Jimi Hendrix, the hippy dude and virtuoso guitarist who stretched the boundaries of youth culture by preaching free sex and the use of drugs. The new territory to be explored became known as 'inner-space', a concept introduced by J G Ballard in *New Worlds* issue 118, which implies an existentialist condition that explores real life experiences such as alienation, sexuality, drug trips and psychosis. Moorcock was obsessed with the ambition to celebrate inventive, radical and relevant writing, which would go beyond the limited genre of science fiction and cross over into literary and, more importantly, popular culture.

Ballard's subsequent world-renowned success is mostly due to Moorcock's tenacity and faith in his early experiments. Ballard has only positive comments to make about his friend: "Mike was a great editor and *New Worlds* under his editorship was the most important literary magazine of the sixties." Another contributor and critic, John Clute, said that whilst Moorcock was full of "elated youthfulness", nevertheless, *New Worlds* was an important "nutrient tank" adding a rich texture to a confused sixties culture. Whilst not all the stories were wholly successful, the magazine as a whole was clearly a catalyst for a paradigm shift in science fiction, if not for late twentieth century British literature.

The New Wave occurred in London in the early sixties with Moorcock encouraging the popularity of arts like rock music, comics and fine art, and there was a link between *New Worlds* and the infamous underground magazines *Frendz, Oz* and *International Times.* Moorcock printed the writing and artwork of Mervyn Peake, the poetry of George MacBeth and published *Entropy* by Thomas Pynchon for the first time in England. It was also *New Worlds* that introduced the art of M C Escher to Britain in 1967. Regular contributors included authors now respected in their own right: Ballard, Brian Aldiss, D M Thomas, Thomas M Disch, John Brunner, M John Harrison, Samuel R Delany, Gene Wolfe, Harry Harrison, Robert Silverberg, Christopher Priest and Robert Holdstock. Terry Pratchett's first story, 'Night Dweller' was featured in 1965 and

Moorcock also accepted an early story by William Gibson. In its changing fortunes over a decade, *New Worlds* received an Arts Council grant, but the magazine was also banned by W H Smiths and mentioned in parliament for the salacious content of one story, "Bug Jack Barron" by Norman Spinrad, now a well-known novel.

In his study of science fiction writers, *Science Fiction: Ten Explorations*, literary scholar C N Manlowe interpreted the 'New Wave' in the following way: *"New Worlds* under the editorship of Michael Moorcock aimed to break down the 'genre' fence of science fiction and while still retaining its imaginative and technical licence with 'reality', make it capable of effects which would give it authority as literature in its own right."

It seems that the development of sf itself owes much to what Brian Aldiss calls, "the Moorcockian revolution." Moorcock with his radical *New Worlds* editorial policy subverted traditional sf expectations, believing instead, as he wrote in issue 151, that: "SF is simply imaginative fiction. It is speculative about science, religion, art, anything treated in a fresh and imaginative way ... The emphasis can be psychological, sociological, metaphysical, the treatment can be surrealistic, realistic or deliberately extravagant."

Whilst the experiments came under a great deal of criticism, Moorcock continued to emphasise the importance of the magazine. Looking back, he has commented that *"New Worlds ...* was not merely its graphics, its articles, its controversies, or, indeed, its fiction. It was an ambience ... a revolutionary and stimulating period." Fantasy and science fiction have never quite been the same since.

Moorcock's own stories were some of the most original and experimental. He began by writing with Barrington Bayley, but soon developed his own individual style. Once installed as editor he took to using pseudonyms for his own contributions, the most common being James Colvin and William Barclay.

Instead of referring to the universe, Moorcock coined the term 'multiverse' to describe the overlapping alternate worlds and realities that his characters inhabit. The concept was introduced in the 1962 story 'Sundered Worlds', published in *Science Fiction Adventures* magazine (the story also became a novel, aka *The Blood Red Game*) to describe multiple universes and planes of existence, which run concurrently and where alternative times and realities co-exist and occasionally interact. The protagonist, Renark, explains the theory of the 'multiverse' as "the multi-dimensional universe containing dozens of different universes, separated from each other by unknown dimensions."

Moorcock himself defined his multiverse as a "near-infinite nest of universes, each only marginally different from the next ... where 'rogue' universes can take sideways orbits, crashing through the dimensions and creating all kinds of disruptions in the delicate fabric of multiversal space-time." Sometimes the planes and times intersect, and various characters, such as Edwardian traveller, Oswald Bastable (one of E Nesbit's 'Treasure Seekers' grown up), join the League of Temporal Adventurers who have learnt to travel across time and space.

'The Time Dweller' (1964) appeared in *New Worlds* before Moorcock became its editor and it tells how the Scar-faced Brooder learns how to manipulate time, so that he can shift between planes or 'time-streams'. This is an important concept in many later Moorcock novels, not least the Jerry Cornelius series and Oswald Bastable trilogy. In a follow up story, 'Escape from Evening' (1965), we learn more about the Time Dwellers who "are capable of moving through time as others move through space." The central time stream through our own universe is called the 'megaflow'.

Moorcock's use of alternate worlds began in the story 'The Pleasure Garden of Felipe Sagittarius' (1965). This presents readers with a version of earth in which Hitler is a captain in the Berlin police working under Bismarck, and Einstein is "an embittered old mathematics teacher." Moorcock continues to be keen to portray "the infinity of possible realities, each subtly different, which exist throughout the multiverse, that decidedly non-linear celebration of our own marvellous minds."

The richest example of Jungian fiction, full of archetypal and mythical symbolism, in *New Worlds* came in the shape of the story, 'The Golden Barge' (written as an unpublished novel in 1957, condensed into a short story in 1965, and finally published as a novel in 1979). The narrative, which has an elusive dream-like quality that owes something to Mervyn Peake, presents Jephraim Tallow distracted from his destiny to follow the mysterious and eponymous barge. He is tempted away by a woman whose love seems perfect until he is driven to kill her. In this exploration of both sexuality and human motivation,

Moorcock employs ornate language and dense psychological symbolism that makes his writing stand above much else that was written at the time.

Tears painted his face in gleaming trails, he was breathing quickly, his brain in a tumult, a dozen emotions clashing together, making him powerless for any action save speech. He gave in suddenly, ashamed for her degradation. He sank down beside her, taking her wet, heaving body in his arms and in sympathy with her grief. And so, locked together in their fear and their bewilderment, they slept.

'The Deep Fix' (1963) was published in sister magazine, *Science Fantasy*, and is an important contribution to that sub-genre of fiction that explores altered states of consciousness. A research scientist named Seward uses hallucinogenic drugs to travel inside his own mind to discover a formula that will save the sanity of the earth's population. Moorcock considered this to be a key story, naming his own rock band after it. It also links Moorcock with American writers such as William Burroughs and Philip K Dick, who were also openly discussing the use of drugs and their effects upon human perception. 'The Deep Fix' interrogates the infinite conundrum regarding dreams, fantasy and reality by asking the essential question; who knows what is real?

If the two main themes of the *New Worlds* writers were psychology and sexuality then nowhere was this more powerfully explored than in Moorcock's story, 'Behold the Man' (1966), which was developed into a novel in 1969. Whilst the short story is powerful, the novel expands the ideas even further and is worth examining as a significant result of the New Wave experiment. *Behold the Man* subverts the Christian salvation story by casting an ordinary, flawed mortal in the role of Christ. It is a disturbing expression of Moorcock's mistrust felt towards religious authority.

The protagonist of *Behold the Man* is Karl Glogauer, a twentieth century Jew whose fantasies confuse religious icons with sexual obsessions. Throughout the novel, Glogauer's mind becomes as fragmented as the text itself. After discovering that "time is nothing to do with space – it is to do with the psyche" he chooses to go back in time to meet Jesus Christ. Glogauer is at first forced to reject his own identity and take on the mantle of the Messiah himself, after being shocked at discovering that Jesus of Nazareth is merely a gibbering imbecile. In a schizophrenic passion "Karl Glogauer entered Christ and Christ entered Jerusalem." As he acts out the role he begins to enjoy the self-importance of becoming Saviour of Mankind and Glogauer's motive is a very real need for some kind of personal identity.

The text is made up of dual narratives, jumping from earlier memories of sexual and intellectual frustrations to his arrival in Jerusalem. The irony becomes more complex and involved as we hear Glogauer in the twentieth century debating the existence of Christ and stating "I'm not a martyr." Yet it seems to be his destiny. As he takes on the messiahship, he remembers back to the twentieth century when his psychologist girlfriend, Monica, had left him a note with the words, "Christianity is just a new name for a conglomeration of old myths and philosophies. All the Gospels do is retell the sun myth and garble some ideas from the Greeks and Romans." He is unaware that he too will continue the cycle – once more reinventing the 'messiah myth'.

In a discussion with Monica, Glogauer states, "Jung knew that the myth can also create the reality." The question being asked is – does it matter if the death and resurrection of Christ are true or is it the symbolism that is relevant? In this respect, Karl Glogauer has both created the myth and been drawn into it, because he believed that humanity needed it to be true. He took the responsibility or at least indulged in the power it would bring, believing that a counterfeit Christ was better than no Christ at all. At least the myth would be there for people to put their faith in and perhaps faith in a myth is preferable to having no hope at all. Moorcock does not deny the truth of the crucifixion but rather admits its necessity for mankind, whether genuine or not. The symbolism of the cross transcends its historical veracity.

Glogauer is himself an amateur psychologist and he realises that he can cure hysterical symptoms and neuroses, showing how the twentieth century understanding of medicine and illness has led to different conclusions and understandings of what once were explained as miracles. Psychology, it seems, has become the new religion, or at least, the theology, of post-modern society and Moorcock offers a psychological interpretation of spiritual healing. "Many he could do nothing for, but others, obviously with remediable psychosomatic conditions, he could help. They believed in his power more strongly than they believed in their sickness. So he cured them."

His radical psychological framework is an exploration and realisation of the existential beliefs that theologian Don Cupitt calls modern Western Christians to in his book, *The Sea of Faith*: "This task of working out a vision of God takes the more human and concrete form of framing a personal vision of Christ, who is our own ideal alter ego, our true Self that we are to become, our religious ideal actualised in human form."

Glogauer in *Behold the Man* lives out this self-realisation and offers the extreme example. This does suggest that we create our own gods, demons and heroes; our own hopes and despairs; our own law and chaos. Moorcock remains optimistic and hopeful with his agnostic belief that love conquers death.

The stark ending of *Behold the Man* offers no answers or solutions and the novel avoids didacticism, preferring to ask questions. The character of Glogauer is a bigot and not a sympathetic character. Moorcock had a challenging aim, which he explains in *Death Is No Obstacle*: "I hope to suggest to the reader that we all share some responsibility for the world's ills ... Glogauer is something of a victim and product of his society, but it doesn't excuse anything he does".

The themes of fate, time, psychology and sexuality explored in *New Worlds* were developed further in Moorcock's works that have become collectively known as 'The Tale of the Eternal Champion'. Through this interconnected series of novels, trilogies and tetralogies Moorcock expounds his philosophical dualism of law and chaos and expands his concept of what he termed the multiverse. Closely related to his concept of the 'multiverse' is that of the Eternal Champion.

3: THE ETERNAL CHAMPION

The Eternal Champion is the generic name for all the incarnations of the one hero who appears in different novels, in different times and places, in various guises throughout the multiverse. Within the entire cycle of novels, known collectively as 'The Tale of the Eternal Champion', Moorcock's different characters, themes, settings and plots overlap through a conscious internal-referencing and intertextuality. Moorcock's fantasies are all interconnected through the various avatars of the Eternal Champion: an everyman hero who fights either chaos or law on behalf of humanity. The best known are those from his sword and sorcery fantasies – Elric the albino; Erekosë the immortal; Corum, the prince in the scarlet robe and Hawkmoon with the jewel in his skull – although the term also applies to Jerry Cornelius, von Bek, Oswald Bastable and so many others.

Moorcock in his early heroic fantasies shows a great preference for romantic protagonists, such as Elric, sometimes called the Womanslayer, a tragic hero akin to Charles Maturin's *Melmoth the Wanderer* and Lord Byron's *Manfred*. Elric fits the template of the gothic romantic character type – the demon-lover. The albino prince of Melniboné first appeared in the 1961 story, 'The Dreaming City' in *Science Fantasy* magazine and owed something to Anthony Skene's character, Zenith the Albino. Elric is dependent at first upon drugs and herbs for strength, then later upon a sinister chaos sword, Stormbringer, which being both sentient and vampiric, thirsts for blood and for the souls of any living creature. This acts as a symbiotic relationship in which Elric becomes bloodthirsty in exchange for physical energy. He is a tortured and neurotic character struggling with pain, anxiety and tragedy after killing his lover, Cymoril. Elric is the inversion of the hero archetype: flawed and therefore, ironically, extremely human.

As a homeless mercenary, Elric pursues a number of supernatural quests, evoking elemental spirits, riding dragons and working for Arioch, a god of chaos. On many of his adventures he is joined by the enigmatic character, Moonglum, the eternal companion.

Elric's destiny is to bring balance to a world in which the gods of Chaos and Law are in constant conflict. In the story 'While the Gods Laugh' (1961) Elric expresses the following paradox: "The upholders of Chaos state that in such a world as they rule all things are possible. Opponents of Chaos ... say that without Law nothing material is possible." Before he dies in the novel *Stormbringer* (1965), Elric sees that the world ruled by Law is no different to that ruled by Chaos. Then after asking Sepiriz, an immortal servant of Fate, the meaning of the cosmic balance an ambiguous answer is returned: "Who can know why the Cosmic Balance exists, why Fate exists and the Lords of the Higher Worlds? There seems to be an infinity of space and time and possibilities ... Perhaps all is cyclic and this same event will occur again and again until the universe is run down and fades away ... Meaning, Elric? Do not seek that, for madness lies in such a course." Elric, the Eternal Champion, finally discovers a purpose for living and a reason for his frailty, for it is only in our weakness and sense of the finite that we can have true freedom.

In *Stormbringer* his destiny is revealed explicitly in a vivid dream: "And the cycles turn and spin and intersect at unpredictable points in an eternity of possibilities, paradoxes and conjunctions ... Thus we influence past, present and future and all their possibilities. Thus are we all responsible for one another..." The Elric novels are full of such philosophical introspection interspersed with violent action. The plots follow epic style quests and usually end with a large-scale battle and resolution.

Many of the early Eternal Champion stories were very personal. Moorcock explains today that: "Elric was me (the me of 1960-1, anyway) and the mingled qualities of betrayer and betrayed, the bewilderment about life in general, the search for some solution to it all, the expression of this bewilderment in terms of violence, cynicism and the need for revenge, were all mine." The alienated hero reflected the inner quest of Moorcock himself, who admits to using personal symbolism within the text to express his own obsessions. Certainly, Elric is the character with whom the writer most closely identifies and Moorcock admits to early and youthful attempts at self-dramatisation, wish-fulfilment and catharsis through these fantasy novels.

The material, external multiverse is a projection of the chaos of our own psyche or id. Moorcock believes that, "When we read a good fantasy we are being admitted into the subterranean worlds of our own souls' and his Eternal Champion novels are charged with personal and metaphysical symbolism.

Erekosë was introduced in the first book Moorcock planned to write, *The Eternal Champion* (written in 1957, first published as a novella in 1962), which acts as the opening of 'The Tale of the Eternal Champion' cycle and is probably influenced by Norse and Icelandic myths. The protagonist begins as John Daker in the twentieth century, but has to learn a new identity as Erekosë, a demi-god, cursed to always be aware that he is more than one person and in visions sees his other avatars. Erekosë is the most unfortunate as he is the one who can see his own destiny and feel the pain of every incarnation. He is pulled through time and space to enter an eternal cycle and never know peace. In the revised version of *The Eternal Champion* (Millennium 1992) Moorcock added the names of other champions to develop the interconnections: "Was I John Daker or Erekosë? Was I either of these? Many other names – Corum Jhaelen Irsei, Aubec, Sexton Begg, Elric, Rackhir, Ilian, Oona, Simon, Bastable, Cornelius, The Rose, von Bek, Asquiol, Hawkmoon – fled away down the ghostly rivers of my memory." The author states that the book "forms the chief rationale and central metaphor to my fiction" and acts as the key to all his heroic fantasy writing.

The most tormented of the champions, Erekosë, expresses this truth when he claims the right to be "free to be the flawed, finite, mortal creatures which from the first was all we ever wished to be." The cycle turns and keeps turning. It is up to the Eternal Champion to make sure the balance is kept in equilibrium lest the world should suffer the legalistic, stifling tyranny of law, or the anarchic insanity of chaos.

Erekosë is conscious of his powerlessness over the destiny that controls him and doomed to never know his true identity. In *Phoenix in Obsidian* (1970), he becomes Urlik Skarsol with a black sword that has similarities to Elric's Stormbringer, and then *The Dragon in the Sword* (1986, and a precursor to *The Dreamthief's Daughter*) sees London born John Daker confronting Hitler in an alternate earth history in which the Nazis become agents of Chaos and Daker and Ulrich von Bek find the Holy Grail. The alternate worlds in these novels are examples of Moorcock's multiverse. The Erekosë novels are written in first person, which make them stand out, and they are the most introspective of Moorcock's heroic fantasies, expressing the anguished thoughts of someone attempting to discover his own identity in a complex world.

Corum comes from the old world of Cornish mythology and his castle at Moidel's Mount is based on St. Michael's Mount near Penzance, which is linked with Arthurian legends. He is an elfin aesthete who desires peace and contentment, but who only learns anger and revenge from the humans, or mabden, who disrupt his life with their hatred and malice. Corum learns that his destiny is to fight for equilibrium and he vanquishes the gods of chaos, Arioch, Xiombarg and Mabelode. He also meets Elric and Erekosë who help to rescue his companion, Jhary-a-Conel from the Vanishing Tower. At the end of the first Corum trilogy in *The King of the Swords* (1972), all the gods of chaos and law are killed and banished leaving an existential utopia where individuals create their own destinies – a state of 'deus abscondis'.

The second trilogy parallels Corum with the Celtic hero Cuchulain, so beloved by W B Yeats. Corum has supernatural powers when his eye and hand are prosthetically transplanted by the eye and hand of twin gods that enable him to see into limbo and call the damned to his aid in his struggle against Prince Gaynor. Explicit references are made to druids and the Sidhe, thus showing how Moorcock was influenced by the Celtic mythologies.

The name Corum Jhaelen Irsei is an anagram of Jeremiah Cornelius; another of Moorcock's eternal champions, from which is also derived Jherek Carnelian and Jhary-a-Conel. He contrives to use many names with the initials J C, which perhaps links his protagonists with the ultimate everyman, Jesus Christ.

Hawkmoon is another gothic romantic hero, being a prisoner of war, initially controlled by the enemy but eventually awakening to individuality. The balance is symbolised by the talismanic Runestaff and is served by the mysterious Warrior in Jet and Gold, a character whose motives and status are ambiguous and who also appears in the Corum novels. He works for fate, like Sepiriz in the Elric mythos.

The first four novels, beginning with *The Jewel in the Skull* (1967) and known as 'The History of the Runestaff', explain how Hawkmoon is controlled by a jewel and how he fights the evil empire of Granbretan, aided by the mysterious supernatural powers of the Runestaff. The Hawkmoon books are perhaps the most stark and barbaric of Moorcock's fantasies. It becomes clear that this is Europe in a post-apocalyptic, primitive future and, ironically, London (Londra) has become an anarchic city of savages set against a German hero. The books are full of vivid descriptions of pagan rituals, futuristic flying machines and the memorable Emperor who is a foetus enthroned in a womb-like globe.

There are games for the reader to play and much fun can be had spotting the bastardised names of real places, such as Kroiden (Croydon), and names of famous British twentieth century politicians, such as "Chirshil … and Aral Vilsn" (Churchill and Harold Wilson). There are even references to some of his own friends, such as J G Ballard and Brian Aldiss, and also to the Beatles: "Gilded figureheads decorated the forward parts of the ships, representing the terrifying ancient gods of Granbretan – *Jhone, Jhorg, Phowl, Rhunga*".

The final three Hawkmoon books are referred to as 'The Chronicles of Castle Brass' and they conclude the entire complex 'Tale of the Eternal Champion' cycle. *Count Brass* recounts the defence of Castle Brass in a medieval alternate France, a land of hope and romance. In *The Champion of Garathorm*, Hawkmoon turns into Queen Ilian, a heroine at last.

In the final novel, *The Quest for Tanelorn*, Elric, Erekosë, Corum and Hawkmoon physically unite to make a creature called 'The Four Who Were One' and in this guise, the Eternal Champion experiences a moment akin to enlightenment when he confronts the entire multiverse and knows no fear: "For the mind of man alone is free to explore the lofty vastness of the cosmic infinite, to transcend ordinary consciousness, or roam the subterranean corridors of the human brain with its boundless dimensions. And the universe and individual are linked, the one mirrored in the other, and each contains the other." This episode is echoed in the Elric novel, *The Sailor On the Seas of Fate*, which tells the same story, but from Elric's viewpoint.

Tanelorn is Moorcock's equivalent to the Elysian Fields of Greek mythology or King Arthur's Avalon, where even the Eternal Champion might find peace. Tanelorn has the ability to shift between planes and protect itself from the outside threats of law or chaos. In the final chapter of the Eternal Champion cycle, in the novel, *The Quest for Tanelorn* (1975), there occurs the Conjunction of a Million Spheres in which all the champions meet in the city, guided by a child called Jehamiah Cohnahlias (another derived name). A final apocalyptic vision helps explain much of the fantastical symbolism and it becomes clear what the chaos sword of Elric, Stormbringer, and the black jewel of Hawkmoon represent, as both transform into one dark figure: "John ap-Rhyss said calmly, 'In Yel, in the villages, they have a legend of such a creature. Say-tunn, is that his name?' The child shrugged. 'Give him any name and he grows in power. Refuse him a name and his power weakens. I call him Fear. Mankind's greatest enemy'." This had been hinted at in the final paragraph of *Stormbringer*, which is repeated here as Hawkmoon's dream.

The sword and sorcery novels always depict the multiversal struggle between the powers of chaos and law and this dualism is a struggle that must be reconciled to achieve individual, creative or cosmic balance. The scales of balance between chaos and order become a political and even religious symbol in many of Moorcock's fantasy works, and love can only be achieved when the two are in equilibrium.

For Moorcock, 'law' is a representation of reason, the rational, logical side of human nature with its preference for order, facts and organisation; namely Utilitarianism. 'Chaos', on the other hand, is a symbol for human emotion, something akin to romance, which can be associated with mythology, the imagination, or in psychological terms, with the unconscious. Romance is a literature of feelings and sensibilities that allows the existence of the supernatural, such as the great gothic romances of the eighteenth century. Romance is often seen as a form opposed to realism or mimetic fiction.

Moorcock freely admits to purloining some of the imagery of the cosmic struggle from Poul Anderson's fantasy novel *Three Hearts and Three Lions* (1953). In a 1963 essay Moorcock explained his cosmology by including a 'Cosmic Hand' at the top of the chain above gods, elementals, sorcerers, men and beasts. It is up to people to fight to maintain a balance.

The dualism of order and chaos is far more complicated than the traditional dualism of good and evil, which is more simplistic. Moorcock explained in an interview with *Vector*, the critical journal of the British Science Fiction Association, that "Law and Chaos are both attractive, both dangerous, and both become worthless if you push them too far." In the justice system, chaos and law are interdependent. Chaos represents the imagination, danger and passion, whilst law represents science, safety and sterility.

Nietzsche wrote, in *The Birth of Tragedy* (1871), about the tension in Greek tragedy between the wild, chaotic Dionysian urge, which is tempered by the restraint and reason of Apollo, and how both are required to create art or poetry. Moorcock's use of chaos and law follows the same model. It becomes clear that chaos and law, whether as religious imagery, philosophical concept, literary metaphor or even personal spirituality, are states to keep in balance. Both are necessary components of a dualism, which implies not so much that they are opposites, but complementary halves to a whole, like the combination of the masculine and feminine in us all. This is also further symbolised by the symbol of the hermaphrodite that reappears in several of Moorcock's novels (*The Final Programme, The City In the Autumn Stars* or the androgyne in *The Dragon In the Sword*). Balance between the two ideals is the only answer; law is required for communal living, but stifles creativity and chaos inspires art, but brings violence and loss of security. Humans need to be emotional and artistic, but if they are to be communal animals then it demands conforming to some agreed consensus.

In Moorcock's sword and sorcery novels spiritual warfare is shown in apocalyptic and surreal visions of worldly battles between creatures and men (most incarnations of the Champion are men, except Ilian of Garathorm and later, the Rose) where, typically, the hordes of chaos are massing for a final confrontation against law. The Eternal Champion fights on whichever side needs help to counteract the flux or entropy (the loss of energy and order) and to create equilibrium. The Cosmic Balance is the overarching power, which controls fate, and the Balance is the closest Moorcock gets to explaining the role or existence of God. It is the cause for which the Eternal Champion is doomed to fight against his will, and this Balance is often represented at the end of a novel by a pair of scales projected upon the heavens. Moorcock suggests that humans are not necessarily fallen or sinful, but are individuals, who are essentially self-responsible, who need rules and routine as well as the chaos of freedom to lead a sane, balanced existence.

Gods, it seems, are merely human metaphors; Balance, or fate, is multiversal justice, represented by Sepiriz or the enigmatic Warrior in Jet and Gold. If there are no gods, then all responsibility is left with the individual. When Elric opens The Dead God's Book, which contains the truth about the cryptic balance and multiverse, it tragically crumbles to dust in his hands. He concludes, "There is no Truth but that of eternal struggle." Moorcock, here, investigates the concept of determinism and concludes that fate is merely mythical symbolism. The reader is left sympathising with the Eternal Champion in his quest for meaning and personal identity.

In an essay collected in *Sojan* (1977), Moorcock explained his aims in writing the Elric stories: "There is ... no Holy Grail which will transform a man overnight from bewildered ignorance to complete knowledge – the answer is already within him, if he cares to train himself to find it".

Most of the novels that comprise 'The Tale of the Eternal Champion' are early Moorcock novels that follow a visionary sequence. They fit into a complex plan to write one gigantic novel and each one has been carefully structured. Moorcock does not, however, wish to be remembered as a writer of sword and sorcery, and he now boasts that many of these books were written quickly. The Hawkmoon books, for example, were each written in three days and he thought nothing of producing fifteen thousand words a day. In fact, between 1965 and 1975 Moorcock wrote about forty books. The Eternal Champion books were written to a formula, one that he developed and that has been much copied since. The Champions usually embark on a quest for a surrogate holy grail, which will bring harmony to the struggle between chaos and law.

Since 1989, however, Moorcock's heroic fantasy novels have been more considered and written in a more literary style, particularly *The Fortress of the Pearl* (1989), which introduces Oone the Dreamthief, and *The Revenge of the Rose* (1991) both of which continue the Elric saga. *The Revenge of the Rose* saw the Rose added to the pantheon, who has since appeared in the Second Ether trilogy (beginning with *Blood*, 1994) and *King of the City* (2000). She is the strongest female Eternal Champion and is related to the von Bek family, discussed in Chapter Eight along with the 2001 novel, *The Dreamthief's Daughter.*

The author has developed a metaphysical cosmology building into a gigantic interconnected mythology. The conscious self- and cross-referencing of the author is often only a code for the initiated and devoted reader. The same characters appear in different contexts, so Wheldrake the poet can accompany Elric as well as exist in the court of Gloriana. Moorcock wants to see how the same character responds in contrasting situations and ages. Elric becomes al Rikh in *King of the City*, and Count Ulrich von Bek in 'The Ghost Warriors' (*Tales from the Texas Woods*, 1997) and in *The Dreamthief's Daughter.*

The Eternal Champion fights the ubiquitous battle of Law versus Chaos and these fantasy novels raise teleological issues leaving the reader with the existential conclusion that we are the masters of our own destiny. Moorcock explained it succinctly on his question and answer website: "If I was God and wanted to make an experiment, I'd set it up pretty much as it is now – and free will would be crucial to the system – because free will invents solutions to problems better than anything else. So if I wanted to make a self-sustaining system, I suppose this is the kind I'd make and non-interference and free will would have to be built into the rules. Therefore I see the world as a self-sustaining organism, at least ideally. It's up to us to make the best of it."

4: Jerry Cornelius

The character of Jerry Cornelius first appeared in *New Worlds* in 1965 as a fragment of what would eventually become *The Final Programme* (1968), after which the next three main novels were published: *A Cure for Cancer* (1971), *The English Assassin* (1972) and *The Condition of Muzak* (1977), and then all four were anthologised as *The Cornelius Quartet* in 1993. The entire Cornelius sequence is, however, more than these four novels and includes a number of spin-off novels and innumerable stories, although not all by Moorcock. The 1971 anthology of Cornelius stories, *The Nature of the Catastrophe*, included stories by Brian Aldiss, M John Harrison and Norman Spinrad, which may make the Jerry Cornelius mythos one of the first 'share-worlds'. The figure of Jerry Cornelius became an iconic cartoon-strip character in the famous underground magazine *International Times (IT)*, drawn by Mal Dean, with R Glyn Jones as co-artist, and written by Moorcock with M John Harrison. Jerry Cornelius reappeared in the 1998 DC comic series 'Michael Moorcock's Multiverse', and in various more recent stories, notably 'The Spencer Inheritance', (*The Edge*, June 1998) referring to the death of Princess Diana and 'Firing the Cathedral' (2002).

With the original four experimental novels, Moorcock captured the spirit of the sixties and seventies through an invocation of street talk, popular fashion, music, promiscuity and pop-culture. Just as jazz inspired the beat generation, so pop music inspired young British writers in the sixties. Moorcock identified with the hipsters, beatniks and particularly the psychedelic hippie movement. Later, his anarchist idealism lead to support of the punk movement, and to his writing a Jerry Cornelius novel *The Great Rock 'n' Roll Swindle* (1980), which tied in with the Sex Pistols' film of the same name. Two comic spin-offs, *The Chinese Agent* (aka *Somewhere In the Night*, 1966) and *The Russian Intelligence* (aka *The Printer's Devil*, 1966) are spoof detective novels following the investigations of one Jerry Cornell.

The literary scholar Mikhail Bakhtin writes about carnival celebrations in *Rabelais and His World*, when he explains how "For thousands of years the people have used these festive comic images to express their criticism, their deep distrust of official truth, and their highest hopes and aspirations." In sixties and seventies Britain, pop culture became the modern form of carnival and an expression for individual freedom. Moorcock successfully utilised this mood, capturing the spirit of the times. It is this optimistic and rebellious spirit that pervades the entire Jerry Cornelius mythos.

Although the four main Jerry Cornelius novels seem anarchic, they are actually very carefully structured in four parts; exposition, development, recapitulation and coda. The three unities of time, place and action are fractured, as is the realistic notion of character development with the characters frequently changing role or personality. The plot for each novel is non-linear and episodic, being more concerned with mood and colour, like music or an expressionist painting.

The tetralogy creates an illusion of surrealism and randomness, but its carefully devised structure uses internal referencing and the use of regular motifs and repetitions. Like the alien worlds of much fantasy and science fiction literature, the world of Jerry Cornelius has its own internal logic. Moorcock wanted his audience to be active and questioning, as he explained in 1976; "Part of my original intention with the Jerry Cornelius stories was to 'liberate' the narrative; to leave it open to the reader's interpretation as much as possible – to involve the reader in such a way as to bring his own imagination into play'.

The world inhabited by Jerry Cornelius, his family, friends and foes is one drenched in the pop culture of sex, drugs and rock 'n' roll, with all three frequently indulged in at wild parties. The language is street talk of the sixties and seventies where people are 'kinky', and are judged by their sexuality and outward appearance whilst a constant soundtrack of jazz, blues and rock music plays in the background. Jerry listens to Zoot Money, The Beatles, Jimi Hendrix, and Hawkwind and is lead guitarist of The Deep Fix. It is here that reality and fantasy merge as the reader wonders how autobiographical Moorcock is attempting to be. Jerry is not merely an autobiographical reflection of Moorcock, but he certainly represents Moorcock's early hedonistic wish-fulfilment to live a life of sensuality and adventure.

To appreciate the Jerry Cornelius books the reader should be well-versed in pop culture. Like many of Moorcock's novels they are post-modern texts that satirise modern culture and express chaos and fragmentation in an increasingly pluralistic world. Through pastiche, collage and parody, Moorcock attacks religion, politics, war and morality and replaces them with the decadence of the emerging popular culture.

The first Jerry Cornelius novel, *The Final Programme* (1968), begins as a conscious rewrite of two Elric stories, 'The Dreaming City' and 'While the Gods Laugh' [both 1961]. Moorcock explains that "in late 1964, I was casting around for a means of dealing with what I regarded as the 'hot' subject matter of my own time – stuff associated with scientific advance, social change, the mythology of the mid-twentieth century. Since Elric was a 'myth' character I decided to try to write his [Jerry Cornelius'] first stories in twentieth century terms."

This translation works effectively and the parallel is explicit. A direct comparison of both openings reveals a group waiting for each Champion. A band of mercenary warriors wait for Elric to lead them to raze his old kingdom city of Imrryr, whilst some scientists await Jerry Cornelius to lead them to his father's post-modern chateau to find a secret microfilm.

The descriptions of the two incarnations of the eternal champion present clear similarities. Elric is the albino wizard-Emperor whose "bizarre dress was tasteless and gaudy and did not match his sensitive face and long-fingered, almost delicate hands'; in comparison, Jerry Cornelius is graceful and mysterious – "He was very tall and the pale face framed by the hair, resembled the young Swinburne's." The choice of Swinburne is interesting as he, like Moorcock, was a bohemian writer; and there is no doubt that Elric and Jerry are shadows of this author.

Instead of being a magician, like Elric who can conjure elementals, Jerry is an ex-Jesuit who has lost his faith. Drugs have replaced magic in terms of altering perception and casting fantastical spells upon the mind. Music and sex have also replaced magic and superstition as ways of transforming the self and overcoming entropy.

Other comparisons are clear: Yyrkoon the evil sorcerer has become Jerry's brother Frank; Cymoril, Elric's only love, is now Catherine, the sister with whom Jerry has an incestuous relationship; even Elric's faithful old retainer, Tanglebones has been anagrammatised into John Gnatbeelson, the butler. Elric fights with his chaos sword that sucks the souls and life force from its victims giving strength and energy to its wielder and similarly, Jerry kills opponents with his unique and mysterious needle gun, a powerful hypodermic full of deadly narcotics, and we discover that he strangely feeds off others in a vampiric sense never fully explained.

A study of the language shows the change in style from romance to post-modern parody. Elric's confrontation with his adversary has him using archaic magic to open a door – "I command thee – open!" which for Jerry has become the sardonic challenge, "Throw in your needle and come in with your veins clear." Next, the albino prince summons Arioch, duke of chaos to protect him, but Jerry makes do with a 'nerve gas grenade' having much the same effect. LSD gas and conventional guns have replaced gods and demons.

Europe becomes "a boiling sea of chaos" made of "fragments of dreams and memories" reminiscent of landscapes traversed by Elric or Corum. Chaos and random flux create a maelstrom of disorder as time begins to run out in a world crying out for a messiah. Elric flies off on the back of a mighty dragon whilst Jerry poses in a Duesenberg limousine, dressed like a pimp.

Jerry is an icon of popular culture: a comic book secret agent or spoof James Bond, as well as a 'cool' rock musician. But he is also a parody of a messiah seeking only the solace of a womb-like enclave where he is protected from each catastrophe. He rejects his status as popular hero for the preferred life of drugs and decadence and lives in the London of the 1960s where the myth of happiness is dominant:

"London was alive with flowers … their scent hung like vapour in the beautiful air. And people were wearing such pretty clothes, listening to such jolly music; the first ecstatic flush of a culture about to swoon, at last, into magnificent decadence, an orgy of mutual understanding, kindness, tolerance." Jerry himself becomes a symbol of this disposable age. He is a victim of fashion, dressed in the costume to suit his role or mood and his identity is signified by his changing fashions and attire, paralleling the fickle pop stars who regularly change their image with each passing trend.

As the incarnation of the Eternal Champion in the modern era, Jerry represents chaos with his rebellious and ambiguous sexuality. "It was a world ruled by the gun, the guitar and the needle, sexier than sex, where the good right hand had become the male's primary sex organ."

Jerry is a self-styled 'Messiah of the Machine Age' and his physical merging with his adversary Miss Brunner in *The Final Programme* is intended to create a true messiah: the ultimate being. However, the plan is doomed to failure and the irony intended is made explicit when a beautiful hermaphrodite emerges from its computerised womb, its first words being the absurd greeting, "Hi, fans!" Rather than being god-like, the hermaphrodite becomes a parody of the androgynous figure of 'camp' pop popularised by David Bowie and his chameleonic characters.

The novel ends with bathos as the 'messiah' drowns all its followers and considers this to be "A very tasty world." This becomes a comment on society's need for messiahs and heroes, and presents the dangers and futility of hero-worship or the self-destructive element inherent in much fundamental religion.

The film of *The Final Programme*, released in 1973, was originally meant to star Mick Jagger, but instead the lead role was given to Jon Finch. In the final scene, instead of a hermaphrodite, the emerging creature is a Neanderthal, presumably representing the regression of mankind's evolution. Moorcock now disassociates himself from the film, which like the novels seems dated, but it is far too limp-wristed to do Moorcock's powerful novel any justice.

The second Jerry Cornelius novel, *A Cure for Cancer* [1971], is darker than the first, with its lengthy descriptions of war-torn cities leaving societies and individuals victims of loss and alienation.

Moorcock is interested in exploring how people and institutions confront the breakdown of order. He describes the structure of *A Cure For Cancer* in the following way. "It starts with the diagnosis of the problem: here is a society in decay ... The chapters get shorter, the rhythm gets more staccato." Like a tune, the plot has different moods and shapes, climaxing in the middle and then fading after a sequence of riffs and melodies. The underlying motif is once more that of entropy and its effect on plot and character. Tragically, there is no cure.

As the Eternal Champion, Jerry Cornelius is resurrected and has become a negative image of himself, with ebony skin, black teeth and long, white hair. He has become a symbolic figure, transcending the constraints of morality and of physics by being free to resurrect himself and to travel through time and space at will. Although free, he questions and seeks his identity, playing a multitude of roles whilst his stories read like nightmares or bad trips, full of guilt and neurosis.

A dandy assassin inhabiting a science fiction landscape, he now owns a 'shifting' machine that unlocks the megaflow of the multiverse allowing its operator to travel through the time streams. When activated it exposes "all layers of existence at once" and seems to need rock music to energise it. The shifter creates webs that lead to all the alternative existences, which are being played out concurrently. This is the 'megaflow' described as moonbeam roads, which weave a web between the alternate worlds. Jerry's black box diffuses and randomises, transporting individuals into another time or plane, which always brings new hope and possibilities.

Jerry remains an agent of chaos, bringing anarchy with his attempts at sabotage and battles against conventionality. The word 'astatic' is used by Moorcock to describe the flux and disorder created by the constant conflict. His opponents represent order and institution, particularly the grotesque Bishop Beesley who slows down time and rides his 'utopia machine' in an attempt to relocate "the virtues of the past." For Beesley, law and order can only come about through suffering. Likewise, Jerry's brother Frank suggests that "We must limit imagination" to regain organisation and stability – a plea that might horrify some, but still reminds us how our society can stifle creativity.

In *A Cure For Cancer*, Moorcock parodies 'order' in his portrayal of the US army who have become Nazi-like dictators, whilst a character called Himmler is merely a seedy night-club owner. General Cumberland's speech about the marines leading Europe into war with their "American strength, American Manhood, ... American bullets ... American virility" is a satirical comment on the Vietnam War – a reality in the background when the novel was written. Moorcock distances himself and the reader from the true horror through his use of comedy, but makes a direct political point, as Moorcock himself explains, "I was substituting England for Vietnam, to bring the war home; to say the same awful distortion of ideals could occur here and we could be its victims." Moorcock parodies a particular American attitude; a militant xenophobia against communism, homosexuality and liberalism, which considers these things as cancers that must be 'cured'. Moorcock is commenting on modern imperialism and the headings to chapters illuminate this point, including a paragraph from Hitler and an advert for a toy Polaris submarine. For Moorcock, order is the domain of the military, the church and science, whilst chaos finds its energy in music, parties and drugs.

Eventually, London is destroyed with napalm and through chemical warfare until in the final quarter of the novel Jerry remembers his only reason for continuing – "There's some hope ... There's a chance of love" and looking once more upon Catherine's body in the morgue, he manages to temporarily reanimate her with his own body heat. In the coda Jerry and his sister's lovemaking melts the snow in a romantic finale, before she dies once more. Love is the only diversion left for Jerry and the only activity that interests him.

Jerry's reality is disturbingly mutable, but his is the world we all experience, one of passions, chaos, fear, 'bad trips' and guilt. The dissipating world in *A Cure For Cancer* echoes the frustrations and emotions in our own minds. The war-torn world is beyond Jerry's power to save, so he turns to individualism and the saving of Catherine, and thus the moral of the story is that for every person the world is only what inhabits the individual mind.

The third novel, *The English Assassin* [1972] is subtitled 'A Romance of Entropy', and gives a detailed, if non-chronological account of the slow demise of an alternative Edwardian Britain where a technological utopia has fragmented into a dystopian pantomime.

Britain is gripped in the 1900–75 war where the air is filled with zeppelin airships whilst music-hall singers entertain at the end of every pier. This was the beginning of a literary trend termed steampunk, a style more fully developed by Moorcock in *A Nomad Of The Time Streams*, later popularised by authors like K W Jeter and Tim Powers.

Within *The English Assassin*, various alternatives are offered, often regressing into decay and destruction or celebrating a *fin-de-siècle* decadence. Moorcock dismantles the logical sequence of the narrative, so that it becomes episodic and ambiguous. Here lies the essence of his multiverse: being able to see many possibilities at once.

Whilst the first two Cornelius books are dynamic and splintered, the last two books have a slower pace, representing entropy – the slow heat death of the universe. Moorcock quotes Rudolf Clausius' famous discovery in 1865 that "the entropy of the universe tends to a maximum", and the Jerry Cornelius novels are an attempt to describe this disintegration with his fragmented prose, in an attempt to uncover "the nature of the catastrophe." The new themes were best served by a new metaphor borrowed from thermodynamics and psychology: the concept of entropy. For the *New Worlds* writers it became a metaphor for the breaking down of conventions and structures. Science writer James Gleick, in his popular book, *Chaos*, defines entropy as "the inexorable tendency of the universe, and any isolated system in it to slide toward a state of increasing disorder." Entropic fiction tends to emphasise alternate states of mind, whilst subverting the conventions of character, plot, time and space.

For Moorcock, entropy equally applies to people, places and time. Entropy represents the inevitability of death and decay, but many of his novels, particularly those exploring the Cornelius mythos, demonstrate how humans overcome death and attempt to create the best quality of life from what they have. This provides something of an existentialist philosophy. Death has lost its sting for Jerry Cornelius who never dies but is continually reincarnated within the multiverse.

Jerry Cornelius is strangely absent in the third book, suffering from catatonia and hydrophilia, he has spent a year or more in a box under the sea. He is a smelly bundle washed up on the seashore, still alive and conscious, screeching and looking like 'a mad gull'. The book is content to follow more closely the other characters of the melodrama as they ship Jerry's body to Dubrovnik, making his body the grail that initiates the adventure. It was with this episode that Moorcock believes he predicted the horrors of the Dubrovnik corpse boats in the Balkan civil war.

Britain itself in *The English Assassin* is a victim of chaos, falling into entropy, disintegrating and slowly melting in the intense heat. The character who stands for order is the bumbling Major Nye, with his old school tie, English country garden and his inability to show affection or emotion. He represents the old-fashioned and paternalistic traditions of Empire, Oxbridge and the armed forces, and whose death near the end takes on a significance in terms of how Britain is crumbling and losing its heritage.

Jerry himself is the most ambiguous character, concurrently a sentient corpse in a box, "a rotting creature which had lain amongst the debris and sheep-dung in the gloomy interior of a tower", or a skeleton of a twelve year old boy. Uncertain memories abound with Jerry as a guerrilla storming Wordsworth's cottage or as a child watching his grotesque mother have sex with a stranger "grunting in unison as orgasms shook their combined thirty eight stones of flesh." The most mysterious moments occur when the Cornelius family and friends are enjoying Sunday roast and it seems that Jerry is not present, but there is an unnamed boy who falls asleep and is ignored like the ghost of a dead child. Only Catherine refers to him and knows that he is having a nightmare. The reader is left to presume that this is Jerry himself, appearing like a phantom, the illegitimate child whose adventures, nightmares, trips, time travelling fantasies of espionage and messiahship fill the pages we are reading.

The English Assassin is a gloomy book filled with horror. One of the most disturbing passages describes fellow temporal adventurer Una Persson being gang-raped and the reader is left with no doubt that this world is collapsing physically and morally. The only response Jerry can give is to ignore the catastrophe by contentedly singing to his ukulele before snoozing on the deck of his boat. The final image of the novel is the bombing and destruction of the seaside resort as Catherine waves, "Goodbye England." Jerry, it seems, is not really interested in world affairs and the possibility of global destruction and neither is he particularly concerned with his own messianic status. He only wants a peaceful quiet life away from power struggles and to be alone with Catherine. Jerry, and perhaps Moorcock, has given up hope for England and now the only chance of salvation is to be found in good old-fashioned love.

Moorcock is not a cynic but a romantic and idealist, and when asked to define entropy he explained that "We use up a lot of energy, collapse and grow cold ... I believe in a sense that human love conquers entropy and that you'll find running through a lot of my books." There is always optimism because love and passion are the only remedy for restoring the human spirit.

The Condition of Muzak presents Jerry's finest performance and the novel won the 1977 Guardian Fiction Prize. We are led through another series of episodic personal mythologies including Arthurian allusions, the underworld of Notting Hill and Portobello, world politics and show business encapsulated under the all-encompassing metaphor of the harlequinade. Jerry once again is many things and many people: an anarchist, a lover, a king, and mainly, "the bravest dandy of them all."

Jerry is an indigenous city dweller. "He was never really comfortable unless he had at least fifteen miles of built-up area on all sides." Cities contain tribes, rituals, superstition, territories, violence, magic and folklore. Moorcock's love for London is one that accepts all that is fake and chaotic about it, and is strangely romantic and honest. The city is always Jerry's security, his urban utopia, and in the Carnival Jerry is the King of London but he is only a symbol – no more than that. Like the Saturnalia with its mock king or Lord of Misrule sacrificed to death, so Jerry Cornelius is the sacrifice, the scapegoat for his generation, the clown who is mocked, criticised, blamed and punished as an example. Miss Brunner, his eternal adversary, sneers at Jerry. "He wasn't his world's Messiah ... He was his world's Fool." But this adds up to the same thing.

During one fancy dress party Jerry is "feeling the loneliness most painful when one is among friends" when he complains to a passer-by, "I used to believe I was Captain of my own Fate. Instead, I'm just a character in a bloody pantomime." The characters begin to take on the identities of stock-types from Commedia dell'Arte or the harlequinade: a theatrical tradition that places the same characters in different plays. Actors play one character all their lives and learn set moves, speeches and jokes. Often the performances would be improvised based around ideas and visual comedy. Typical themes included unrequited love, mistaken identity and cuckolding.

Jerry is always hoping to be Harlequin who is quick witted and wily with a huge sexual appetite, but the suggestion that he is only an adolescent dreaming up masturbatory fantasies is implied more strongly. He is, in fact, only Pierrot, the frustrated dolt. It turns out that Una Persson is the real Harlequin and is Catherine's chosen lover, thus becoming Jerry's main rival in love.

Catherine is Columbine, the rational and self-sufficient woman who is the object of most people's desire and who becomes Jerry's only purpose or hope; she provides a genuine love for him to respond to. She is always the catalyst who provokes and sustains the action. Their interdependency is highlighted near the end of the novel when her reflection in a pool shows his face rather than hers.

The unsavoury Bishop Beesley, an agent of law who pursues Jerry throughout the tetralogy, is an amalgam of two Commedia dell'Arte characters – Pantalone and Captain Fracasse who are aggressive and authoritarian. Jerry's brother Frank is Scaramouch, the stirrer and antagonist. All the city folk are playing their roles in the scenario, rehearsing and performing behind their social masks which leads to one of the most colourful set-pieces in *The Condition of Muzak* which celebrates Christmas. Characters in the novel become the stock-types from mummers plays, mystery cycles, pantomime, fairy tales and mythology. Miss Brunner the school Ma'am becomes Britannia, a character Moorcock later identified as a prototype Mrs Thatcher; Major Nye the Imperialist is Saint George; Mrs Cornelius Jerry's mother, is Widow Twanky.

In fact, Mrs Cornelius is one of Moorcock's most bizarre and enduring creations (who also appears in the Colonel Pyat novels). She is a foul-mouthed and grotesque character straight from the works of Dickens or Peake. Jerry appears to be very dependent upon his mother with whom he has an oedipal relationship. She drinks gin, belches and uses expletives unthinkingly, and yet she is always attractive to men. Her reactions are ludicrous and show her to be indomitable, for example during a picnic with her family, her lover is shot before her eyes, but she turns to Frank and comments, "Still, yer've got ter larf, incha?" She is most cynical about Jerry, while he is in stasis in his coffin-like box and yet whilst she does not understand his achievements or his aims, she is incredibly perceptive and the reader understands her attitude when she glibly states, "Iber-bleedin'-natin' 'e corls it! master-fuckin'-batin' I corl it!"

This evaluation of Jerry could well be accurate, and the ambiguity of his character allows this to be a distinct possibility. Moorcock has intimated as much. In fact, the tetralogy ends with a very ordinary scene at the Cornelius' home while Jerry remembers "a bad science fiction film in which he had appeared for a few seconds, as an extra." There is just a chance that the great Jerry Cornelius is just a grubby adolescent escaping into a libidinous, wishful fantasy. Thus he becomes an everyman who experiences all our hopes, dreams, failures and pain. Moorcock once explained that, "Jerry is everything. Everyone."

5: Dancers At The End Of Time

Embraced within the Eternal Champion cycle is another series of novels, *The Dancers At the End of Time*. In these, Moorcock employs comedy, fantasy and an elaborate style straight from the literary *fin-de-siècle* to portray the clash of two cultures. If Jerry is the failed messiah then the other avatar of the eternal champion with the same initials, Jherek Carnelian, is the eternal child – naïve and inquisitive. The three novels *An Alien Heat* (1972), *The Hollow Lands* (1974) and *The End of All Songs* (1976) are now anthologised under the title *The Dancers at the End of Time*. There are also three sequels to the trilogy: *Legends From the End of Time* (1976) consisting of three short stories, a novel called *The Transformation of Miss Mavis Ming* (1977 and which is also a sequel to *The Winds of Limbo*, 1965) and the novella *Elric at the End of Time* (1981), which connects the series more closely to his Eternal Champion cycle. The protagonist is Jherek Carnelian, a derivation of Jerry Cornelius, thus expanding Moorcock's ever-widening multiverse.

The initial trilogy presents a bizarre, satirical and lyrical vision of an anarchist utopian future in which a repressed puritan, Mrs Amelia Underwood, comes into conflict with a promiscuous aesthete, Jherek Carnelian. Once again we get a glimpse of the eternal struggle between law and chaos, this time with comic consequences and a large cast of grotesque characters involved in witty dialogue and black comedy. The style is tragi-comic also owing something to 'nonsense' and absurdism. Moorcock believes that "Comedy – like fantasy – is often at its best when making the greatest possible exaggerations" and these novels contain some of his most extreme and larger than life characters. *The Dancers at the End of Time* is evidence that Moorcock was writing humorous fantasy and science fiction long before either Douglas Adams or Terry Pratchett popularised the forms.

The first novel, *An Alien Heat,* is a comedy of misunderstanding and human error. It begins at the end time of our universe where "the human race had at last ceased to take itself seriously." We are presented with an entropic world where decadence and sensuality dominate the mainstream philosophy giving an immediate parallel to the bohemian Decadence movement. 'The Decadence' refers to a group of subversive writers, such as Oscar Wilde, Charles Baudelaire, Arthur Machen and M P Shiel, who wrote outrageous work around the end of the nineteenth century. Moorcock also acknowledges George Meredith and once again the poet A C Swinburne as influences and this is evident in the ornate language and use of irony and metaphor.

Moorcock creates a culture with new psychological dynamics. There is a question as to whether this society is a utopia or dystopia, but it is certainly a presentation of exaggerated anarchism – that is, freedom from authority and laws. On the positive side this is a society with no problems regarding greed or jealousy, because possessions are unimportant. All desires are freely catered for, and each individual has the power to create any physical object from thin air or fulfil any dream using a ring which allows anything from their imagination to come true. The end of time is an amoral culture in which incest and promiscuity are dull, everyday activities. Jherek regularly consummates his physical love for his mother, The Iron Orchid, as if it were perfectly normal; and for him it is. However, time-travellers from other eras and worlds are predictably horrified.

At the beginning of *An Alien Heat,* Jherek Carnelian and his mother enjoy a picnic on the beach eating sumptuous foods whilst discussing the unfamiliar ideas of 'virtue' and 'self-denial' about which Jherek has read but is uncertain of their meaning. The reader quickly learns that the inhabitants of the end of time are obsessed with abstract experiences and show disinterest and naivety towards concepts like old age, time and death. They are gods grown bored. They all have the power to resurrect anyone who is unfortunate enough to die; otherwise they are immortal, so death has lost its sting and truth or reality is constantly questioned and ambiguous. Jherek asks his mother rhetorically, "...but what is particularly interesting about the truth?" Life has become a vulgar game. A time traveller comments upon their lifestyle – "You play mindless games without purpose or meaning", which sums them up quite neatly. Having no aim or purpose in life creates boredom and ennui.

Like a comedy of manners, *An Alien Heat* involves courting, love, jealousy and witty repartee. The style of language is romantic and the plot uses the traditions of farce to sustain and develop plot lines. The narrative revolves around the unlikely relationship between the innocent, idealistic Jherek and the Edwardian puritanical housewife Mrs Amelia Underwood, who is transported millions of years forward in time. Jherek decides to fall in love with her as an amusing experiment and his lovemaking involves insincere games as he fails to appreciate her different socialised assumptions. Jherek plans their future together in his imagination: "If she fell in love with him tomorrow (which was pretty inevitable, really) there were all sorts of games they could play – separations, suicides, melancholy walks, bitter-sweet partings and so on." The comic ordering of these activities shows his ignorance of true sacrifice, for suicide is just another silly game if resurrection is possible. However, Mrs Underwood's idea of love is also insincere. She speaks proudly of her steadfast commitment to her distant husband and their "institute of Christian marriage", which is lawful even if there is no love involved.

Once again the extremes of chaos and law are distinguished here with a romantic stalemate between a hedonist and an ascetic, two philosophies that Moorcock successfully satirises. Jherek is the bohemian with magical powers and his artistry lacks taste and subtlety whilst Mrs Underwood remains virtuous and is sensible to her 'duty' and dignity. She finds him depraved and corrupt, whilst he is continually confused and frustrated. Mrs Underwood, who has chosen order and stability, sees it as her mission to convert Jherek to her standards. She could be free of her repressed and sheltered upbringing and fulfil all her fantasies and yet she chooses to reject all enjoyment and lead a dull temperate life.

The tone is then set for tragedy until Jherek travels back in time to Edwardian London, following his new-found love. Unfortunately, Jherek there begins to take himself seriously, and mourns his loss of irony with a cry of, "It is no longer a game!" In an uncharacteristic moment of self-realisation he recognises that his love is genuine and this is certainly a new experience that also involves pain.

Moorcock's London is the grimy underworld of Ben Jonson and Charles Dickens, filled with corrupt stock-types and squalid criminals' dens, such as Jones' kitchen, also known as 'The Devil's Arsehole'. Jherek's evaluation of our world is summed up in his cry of disbelief – "many of their pastimes are not pursued from choice at all." Jherek becomes an allegorical figure caught up in crime, and it is only when he is hanged, accused wrongly of murder, that Mrs Underwood finally declares her love for him. The convention of tragedy is subverted when the reader remembers that, for Jherek, death is no obstacle.

The second book in the series, *The Hollow Lands*, makes good use of farce, particularly the sections involving ridiculous sex-crazed aliens and some Keystone Kop-like policemen, creating a manic slapstick style in the tradition of Victorian pantomime, although the novel is not made up of comedy alone.

The greatest moment of realism occurs when Jherek meets the writer H G Wells with whom he discusses time-travel. Wells recognises Jherek as an eloi, one of the aesthetic race of creatures evolved from humans, as described in his novel, *The Time Machine*. It is significant that Wells appears in these novels as time travel is discussed at some length. Back at the end of time their own scientist, Professor Morphail, has invented a time machine, but he describes the paradox and problem for all time travellers. "If one goes back to an age where one does not belong, then so many paradoxes are created that the age merely spits out the intruder as a man might spit out a pomegranate pip which has lodged in his throat." Jherek manages temporary shifts but cannot control his movement like the nomads of the time streams can.

The residents at the end of time, such as Bishop Castle and Gaff the Horse in Tears, become quickly bored with their lives and create different realities depending upon their whims and moods, fashioning houses, new games to play and even whole worlds, all in intricate detail by the use of their energy rings.

There is much aesthetic debate in the novel about the difference between reality, realism and the artistic product. The residents' fake realities are more detailed and preferable to actual reality, although they lack the authenticity of smell and texture. However, Jherek begins to crave a more passionate and chaotic form of expression and Robot Nurse laments the loss of romance. In a moment of Moorcockian self-reference, the author has her quoting from his earlier fantasy, *The Knight of the Swords*, which describes a primeval world of magic and mythology filled with "phantasms, unstable nature, impossible events, insane paradoxes, dreams come true, dreams gone awry, nightmares assuming reality." Here Moorcock seems to be reminding us of the importance of fantasy, which gives us the ability to dream and escape from reality.

The book ends with a discussion regarding self-denial and Jherek still failing to grasp such a pointless concept. With Jherek's final words ("what is 'self denial'?"), which are also the final words of the book, we see that he still has much to learn. The reader is reminded that love is a game in which the chase is more fun than the apprehension.

The End of All Songs continues the courtly dance and, of the trilogy, is the most subtle and graceful with its baroque language and descriptions of elaborate social conventions and leisurely lifestyles. The cycle is concluded with Jherek learning to be unhappy and experiencing jealousy for the first time. He realises that his world is artificial and rediscovers his own humanity. The novel's structure is unusual, beginning with catharsis followed by denouement, resolution and then ending with tension and further development.

The conflict is a continuation of the complex relationship between the ordered discipline of Mrs Underwood who follows the utilitarian ethic that "If one leads a moral life, a useful life, one is happier", and Jherek's libertarian world of freedom and imagination. Moorcock is emphatic in his preference for the latter and eventually even Mrs Underwood begins to question her own beliefs. The culture of Edwardian middle class is parodied for its ridiculous constraints upon natural behaviour and for the repressed anguish and pain caused by these suppressions. Jherek and Mrs Underwood begin to understand each other, as she becomes more sensitive and less callous.

"I love you," he said. "I am a fool. I am unworthy of you."

"No, no my dear. I am a slave to my upbringing and I know that upbringing to be narrow, unimaginative, even brutalising … And now I see that I am on the verge of teaching you my own habits – cynicism, hypocrisy, fear of emotional involvement disguised as self-denial".

Her original intention was to educate these "noble savages", but she ends up admiring their simple honesty.

Whilst chaos implies pleasure, order demands suffering. Mrs Underwood continues to criticise her own world, which we recognise as our own. "You do not know my world, Jherek. It is capable of distorting the noblest intentions, of misinterpreting the finest emotions." Moorcock's critique of Western culture is explicit and as the new Adam and Eve, Jherek and Mrs Underwood have a romantic chance to start the human race again.

Just as carnival comedy ridicules those who represent status and authority, so these novels are full of witty satire and damning black comedy that laughs at the constricting dominant culture. The anarchic culture at the end of time is offered as a more attractive place, full of magic and innocence. The characters are colourful and shocking, like the rebels and beatniks of pop culture who are treated as outcasts by those in the mainstream. There is the morbid gothic romantic, Werther de Goethe who dwells in loneliness and self-pity to live out the archetypal existence of the anguished poet and rejected lover. Mistress Christia The Everlasting Concubine represents the extreme in sexual amorality, willing to try any form of pleasure however perverted.

As Jherek's true father, Lord Jagged of Canaria acts as the catalyst for the entire narrative bringing together the two protagonists and manipulating their actions like a puppet master conceiving jests and fabulations. His role is similar to that of the Warrior in Jet and Gold from Moorcock's Hawkmoon books. He is identified as both Mephistopheles and Machiavelli and also takes on the role of judge in the nineteenth century with the ironically changed name of Jagger, linking him with one of the most subversive pop stars of our own times. These outrageous characters are reminiscent of the hippies of the decade of pop psychedelia. Cosmic irony is evident with Lord Jagged controlling the characters' destinies, manipulating their futures and performing experiments with his friends and family as test-subjects. This theme of God as the archetypal ironist laughing at our expense is one that recurs in Moorcock's work. In the short story,

Elric At the End of Time, it is strongly implied that Lord Jagged is Arioch the god of chaos whom Elric serves.

The Dancers at the End of Time explores the juxtaposition of two cultures, which also represent the notions of classicism and romanticism. Once again, order has a repressive and stifling effect upon its inhabitants, whilst chaos gives room for creativity and artistic endeavour with the added danger of passion and pain, which can also be destructive.

The Dancers at the End of Time is a post-modern montage and pastiche of various modes of writing. Moorcock's visionary novels work on many levels, satirising Protestant morality and comparing it to utopian libertarianism, whilst also experimenting with fantasy and comic forms of literature.

6: GLORIANA

Arguably Moorcock's most literary fantasy, *Gloriana,* which won the World Fantasy Award and the John W Campbell Memorial Award in 1978, owes much to Mervyn Peake's Gormenghast trilogy. Literary scholar Peter Caracciolo described the novel as "that apotheosis of heroic burlesque" and this is certainly an apt summation. It parodies Edmund Spenser's 16th century allegorical poem, *The Faerie Queene,* subverting the romantic literary notions by making a humanist comment on Spenser's moralism. *Gloriana* is not merely a pastiche allegory of Queen Elizabeth I, but is also a dark, psychological exploration of human conflict in which the queen's palace and castle, with its hidden corridors and rooms, represents the mind, riddled with repressed guilt, hypocrisy and corruption. With its themes of chaos versus law, sexuality and its use of depth psychology, this novel can be seen as a consummation of the literary experiment that Michael Moorcock began as editor of *New Worlds.*

    Gloriana, or The Unfulfill'd Queen was first published in 1978 and then revised in 1993 in response to feminist criticism from Moorcock's friend Andrea Dworkin who argued that the climactic, penultimate chapter, as it was originally written, could be seen as a justification for rape. This concerned Moorcock who considers himself a feminist sympathiser, so whereas Queen Gloriana had originally been the victim, her role is switched so that she becomes the violator.

Before this questionable denouement in which Gloriana finally controls the antagonist of the novel, Quire, sexually, she learns of her own shocking conception and that she was raped by her own father, presenting the brutalism of some men who seek sexual power within relationships. This is the worst side of chaos. Moorcock has written articles from a feminist standpoint arguing that "women are constantly and systematically silenced by men, by male-dominated society." In *Gloriana* fulfilment is found when the woman rediscovers her rightful power and the man learns to know fear.

The revision omits two pages (pp375-6 of the 1978 Fontana edition) and adds five new pages (pp362-6 of the 1993 Orion edition). In the original, Quire rapes his Queen and then illogically switches personality as if schizophrenic. "Quire jumped back, careless of his own unfinished pleasure, and his face was suddenly quite innocent." However, in the revised edition Gloriana threatens Quire with a knife between his legs and discovers her own true identity whilst taming Quire, her evil alter ego: "She was no longer Albion. No longer justice, mercy and wisdom, no longer the personification of righteousness, the hope and ideal of her people. She was Glory. She was self... He stumbled back ... The beast cowered for an instant in his eyes before fleeing entirely exorcised, and leaving him looking at her with the awe some ancient hermit might have lavished upon the face of a deity." This gives a better justification for Quire's reversal and strengthens Gloriana's character adding weight to the consummation of chaos and order, and significance to the romantic ending where Quire becomes Arthur in an ideal kingdom of knights and chivalry. The Romantic and Classical traditions finally unite. Moorcock uses the metaphor of the balance to represent renaissance notions of harmony, furthering his motif of the duality of chaos and order.

Gloriana is not an individual, but a symbol who personifies the state of Albion, with "personal decisions subservient to the needs of the state." She is seen to hold the state in equilibrium and balance with all laws and values personified in this one god-like figure. She is deified and yet the reader soon discovers her to be a flawed and sympathetic figure, frustrated sexually with an urge, which it seems will never be gratified, as the novel's subtitle suggests. 'Her Majesty's Curse' is that she cannot achieve release from her burdens through orgasm even through her private decadent and orgiastic experiences. This lack of fulfilment brings her continued torment. Gloriana is neither virtuous nor a virgin, she regularly practices sexual deviance and masochism within her seraglio and has many bastard children, yet she remains unfulfilled.

Gloriana's femininity is essential to the plot and purpose, and is an important part of Moorcock's own philosophy. Whereas traditional masculinity celebrates violence and danger, the Queen rejects such male obsessions, "But I fear war and all that attends it ... Violence simplifies and distorts the Truth and brings the Brute to eminence." The traditional 'feminine' qualities are the strengths required to lead a liberal society.

Gloriana is a woman in a world where all other leaders are men and even her own state is run by men. She has learnt to play her part, but remains only a symbol and not an individual. "She was like a splendid flagship ... cheered on by everyone who watched her glide across the water, and none to know that, below the waterline, she had no rudder and no anchor." Her constant dilemma remains her balancing her monarchy with her humanity. Gloriana loses her individual identity for the sake of her nation, Albion, as her priority lies with her subjects and kingdom, her own satisfaction and wellbeing coming second. Although Gloriana is the main character Moorcock uses the technique of omniscient author, allowing the reader insight into the minds and points of view of other characters.

Captain Quire represents chaos as the amoral libertine who murders, deceives or corrupts all he meets before cheating his way into Gloriana's affections. His name adds a hint of irony, linking him with religion and church, and the narrative use of 'chorus'. The author describes him as "a demon", a malevolent spirit who manipulates and brainwashes people, such as minor characters Alys Finch and Phil Starling, who he tames as little pets. He easily seduces Gloriana, for it is the monarch's raging lust for sexual gratification that allows chaos to disturb the order of Albion. The Platonic ideal of love and unity is corrupted by the selfish pursuit of desire and pleasure.

The Queen's Lord Chancellor, Lord Montfallcon, provides the balance between order and chaos. Whilst Gloriana is the symbolic figurehead, the state's ship is truly steered by this devious politician. Montfallcon is obsessed with maintaining order and tradition, and is dedicated in his love for the queen, whom, we finally discover, is his own granddaughter. Even he admits that peace is a charade; only he knows and plots behind the façade of order, hiding all true corruption and conspiring with criminals in order to maintain the myth of glory and the golden age. Ironically, it is his servant Quire who shatters the veneer of harmony. In shame, Montfallcon recedes into self-immolation and his relapse is part of Albion's downfall. Montfallcon plays a similar role to Lord Jagged and the Knight in Jet and Gold who control the balance through manipulation and artifice.

It is quickly apparent that Albion as a utopia is counterfeit; it is really inhabited by whores and blackguards, and the members of the Privy Council are mere fops. The myth of peace and justice is sustained by regular masques and festivals, which romanticise the reign of Gloriana and help the public to believe in the myth of perfect harmony. Montfallcon is an idealist who wants order by hiding chaos, which, in essence, means the so-called utopia of Gloriana is little different to her own father, Hern's, tyranny. During one episode of unsolved murder, Sir Tancred, one of the Queen's knights, is accused even though he has no motive, nor the temperament, and yet Montfallcon is ruthless in his speculation, seeking to retain order at all costs: "He hoped that Tancred were not innocent. It was better to have a culprit, cut and dried, than a court that simmered in speculation, rumour, gossip, suspicion and fear. He could sense them now, threatening his Golden Age, his Reign of Piety, his Age of Virtue."

Moorcock explains that the palace "represents not only the brain, the conscious and unconscious minds, but behaviour and motivation too." The dark inner passages and secret rooms behind the walls are a metaphor for Gloriana's mind, which has fallen victim to entropy; walls are crumbling, members of the court are bored, entertaining themselves with traditional pursuits and masques. It is almost to relieve the torpor that the Queen accepts the unpopular Quire as her lover, but he brings crime, lust and selfishness into the peaceful 'utopia'. Moorcock suggests that the chaos brought by Quire was a necessary input into a court full of hypocrisy and deception. It is only Quire who brings the Queen and her courtiers to life with his own energy, finally making them look at themselves and their own lives with some honesty. In this sense, Quire is an essential part of each one of us.

Although *Gloriana* is not an historical romance its links with history are clear. Elizabeth I was born a bastard of King Henry VIII and Anne Boleyn, and some historians intimate that Elizabeth was the issue of a rape and possibly violated as a child by the infamous Thomas Seymour. Historians commonly note that her main priority in all her decisions and actions was "the weal of the kingdom" and whilst her famed virginity is questionable, the fact that that she was a strong female leader is undoubted.

Quire seems to be an allegorical amalgamation of two historical characters who disturbed life in Elizabeth's court, namely the Earls of Essex and Leicester; both rogues.

As well as the extensive royal household of over 1500 people, Queen Elizabeth also had other favourites who visited her rooms, including the infamous alchemist John Dee who would cast her horoscope. Doctor Dee was a sixteenth century mathematical philosopher who dabbled in theatrical illusions and magical practices such as astrology, in those days regarded as a common science. In *Gloriana*, Dee, whose name remains unchanged, is secretly and painfully in love with his Queen, comically lusting after her as he talks politely. "He bowed again, sucked in a breath or two. (Blood of Zeus! These pantaloons will make a eunuch of me yet!)." Dee also becomes the mouthpiece explaining Moorcock's beloved multiverse with its intersecting spheres and parallel worlds.

Structurally the novel is based on four theatrical pageants. During the Twelfth Night Festival, Gloriana is presented as Freyja, a facet of the ancient European goddess, Frigg, who was considered a goddess of sexuality and an aspect of the Mother Earth. The poem written by Wheldrake invokes the Norse gods of Asgard and knights re-enact the battle of Fire and Ice, another dualism, before Ragnarok, the last battle, from whose ashes is born the new world and Albion. Ragnarok, also known as the Twilight of the Gods, is both a beginning and an end. It symbolises the birth of a utopia, but also signals the end of order and the coming of chaos. In *Gloriana* Quire is the equivalent of Loki, the mischievous god who brings disorder.

During the Mayday Spring festival, things start to go wrong, but not until we are treated to Wheldrake's Spenserian pastiche called

'Atargatis; or the celestial virgin', adding a new character to Moorcock's complex mythology. Gloriana is the May Queen, another incarnation of Mother Earth also connected with fertility rituals.

The Accession Day Tilt is the chance for a summer tourney with its affirmation of chivalry, where Quire, as Palmerin, the eponymous hero of an ancient European epic poem, becomes the Queen's new champion. As the Court falls further into decadence and entropy, Autumn brings the annual Feast of Bacchus, an orgy to delight all the senses, particularly sexual and visual. The sexual games become more explicit and less tasteful, whilst Gloriana struggles to play her expected roles as Mother, Protector and most difficult, Goddess. Until her moment of individuation she is an automaton manipulated firstly by Montfallcon and then by Quire. Indeed the entire court is led a courtly dance by Quire until all the members of the privy council and the Queen herself are no better than toy-maker Master Tolcharde's clockwork harlequinade. Here Moorcock reminds us of the recurring symbolism of the Commedia dell'Arte in his work, a motif which represents the cyclical lives, deaths and myths which invade the multiverse.

Even though *Gloriana* is a single volume, it cannot escape the boundaries of Moorcock's immeasurable multiverse, and a certain number of familiar names appear within the castle walls. Jephraim Tallow is a minor figure skulking in the shadows, and interestingly, is the protagonist of Moorcock's first novel, *The Golden Barge*, which follows a similarly baroque style and psychological themes. The poet Ernest Wheldrake reappeared in the 1991 Elric novel, *The Revenge of the Rose*, which is also the most "literary" of his sword and sorcery novels in which Wheldrake became Elric's companion on the quest for his father's soul, composing sonnets and odes on heroic and philosophical themes. In *The Dancers at the End of Time* Mrs Underwood quotes a poet called Wheldrake from Edwardian England, and whose verses read like those of Swinburne and Moorcock has explained that "Swinburne attacked himself as Wheldrake." A third recurring character in *Gloriana* is Una, who whilst also a character in *The Faerie Queene*, is undoubtedly related to the immutable temporal adventuress, Una Persson from the Jerry Cornelius and Oswald Bastable series. She certainly represents the most sensible and human side of the female.

Life in the court is tortuously dull, so the characters spend their energy and time amusing and diverting themselves with theatrical entertainments, sexual exploits and political intrigue, until they gradually dissipate, receding into brooding despair. The novel lays down some positive and challenging ideas; not least that life is a precarious balance between virtue and vice, and it is only when these opposites are reconciled do we begin to experience the completeness of our own existence. The sexual union of Gloriana and Quire provides an allegory for the fulfilment of the male and female complement, which has found expression elsewhere in Moorcock's work in the symbol of the hermaphrodite. Life is a sensory experience where desire must be fulfilled and feelings must be expressed, but only in a society where there is some acknowledgement of responsibility and medium of control.

Moorcock, in claiming his own purpose in writing the novel, states something similar: "I was trying, if this doesn't sound too nuts, to reverse the idealising allegory of *The Faerie Queene* and give Gloriana back her humanity. I'm also very fond of Quire. I would say that love, in the form I most admired it, was respect for, and celebration of, the individuality of others."

In Moorcock's novel, the state represents authority, whilst Quire becomes a symbol for the id, particularly the complex desires of the Queen herself. The climax of the revised novel is literally an orgasm, fulfilling the ultimate aim of the carnival, which is the birth of a new world and Quire's coronation is the triumphant crowning of the carnival king. Romance and Classicism finally unite but the ending is just another masque. The final sentence is an echo of the opening, thus completing the cycle of the seasons.

In *Gloriana* the reader is presented with a liberal authority that is paternalistic on the outside but corrupt within – a model familiar to Western politics today with the advent of media manipulating spin-doctors and constant allegations of 'sleaze'. The novel invokes symbolic images of power on both an individual and national scale.

7: Colonel Pyat

The four volumes, which compose the memoirs of Maxim Arturovitch Pyatnitski (Colonel Pyat), are referred to as the 'Between the Wars' sequence and their titles together make a complete saying. *Byzantium Endures* (1981) presents us with Pyat's precocious adolescence and pretentious engineering ambitions as he grows up in Odessa and St Petersburg. The Russian Civil War disrupts his plans and he finds himself unwillingly fighting alongside Makhno, the anarchist revolutionary folk-hero who also appeared in *The Steel Tsar* (1981). In *The Laughter of Carthage* (1984) Pyat gets caught up in the proto-fascist political machinations of 1920s Turkey and Italy before becoming a travelling speaker for the Ku Klux Klan in the United States. *Jerusalem Commands* (1992) evokes the glamour of Hollywood where Pyat stars in silent movies, but during filming in Egypt he is tricked and brutally abused to the point of breakdown, after which he returns to his ideals of creating a technocratic utopia. The final volume *The Vengeance of Rome* examines Pyat's involvement with two of the most frightening tyrants of recent history, Hitler and Mussolini. Pyat had already indicated his sympathy for Mussolini's vision in *Jerusalem Commands*. "Adolf Hitler, representing proud masculinity, and Benito Mussolini, representing the spiritual, feminine side of the fascist discipline. Left alone, I think they would have made perfection." He is a character and narrator with whom it is difficult to empathise.

These are the most consciously political of Moorcock's novels, exploring the uses and misuses of power in the twentieth century. In his system, order is a synonym for tyranny and authoritarian control, whilst chaos symbolises the more liberal theories of individual autonomy and community that is best represented by anarchism, which rejects authority and hierarchy. Moorcock believes that any form of authority, left or right wing, ends up oppressive: "Uncertain of the consequences of genuine social change, nervous of the 'Chaos' manifested through the incoherent euphoria and destructiveness of the mob, leaders of revolutions fall back on the methods of their predecessors in an effort to restore the rule of 'Law'."

The Pyat tetralogy has one distinct voice; the first person narrative of Maxim Pyatnitski, which expresses the opposite views to those held by the author. By his own admission Moorcock had difficulty sustaining the writing, particularly the final novel, *The Vengeance of Rome*, professing that the material was "Hard, dangerous stuff to contemplate." Moorcock clearly rejects the evils of tyranny and campaigns against prejudice and sexism, but has taken on the demanding task of entering the consciousness of a bigot. His disclaimer is made immediately in the introduction to *Byzantium Endures* when Moorcock claims that he merely edits the manuscript of one who is "a liar, a charlatan, a drug addict." This technique of claiming editorship of someone else's work is a device for creating a greater sense of realism and the author has used this technique to good effect in previous novels, particularly the Bastable novels which follow similar themes. Moorcock wants the reader to believe that Pyat is a real person involved in actual historical events, so when Moorcock appeared in an interview in London in 1993 he arranged for an actor playing Pyat to interrupt him from the floor and to take over his 'own' story. Pyat is a character, or at least a name from the Jerry Cornelius books, and is based on a real person from Moorcock's home in Notting Hill, London.

On reading the memoirs, it becomes clear that whilst the young Pyat dreams of scientific progress with his utopian vision of a technocracy, as an older man he has become excessively reactionary and mentally unbalanced. It is the older, schizophrenic Pyat who writes in retrospect and he interrupts his own stream of consciousness with his vitriolic asides 'uttered' in a sometimes impenetrable mixture of English, Russian and Polish, giving the impression that he is shouting directly at the reader. Whilst much of the prose is clearly structured following his unorthodox journeys chronologically, the text is continually disjointed by his wilder and darker passions and it is in these moments that the reader encounters the real man, and confronts his most violent thoughts.

Moorcock uses the distasteful, if sometimes amusing, voice of Pyat to create a distancing for the reader further explaining that, "With each sentence there is the possibility that it is not the truth. So each sentence has to contain or contribute to an ambiguity." The reader is left to make moral choices based on the memoirs of an unreliable narrator.

The novels are a biased history of the terrifying political changes in the twentieth century, particularly those leading into the Russian Civil War and then the Second World War. Pyat, whose racism and invective are forced upon the reader, is an unsympathetic character and an egotist, whose anti-Semitism led to the book being heavily censored in the USA. Pyat also has the ability to continually reinvent himself, and like the Eternal Champion he can be 'resurrected' with a different identity depending on the context. He is more despicable than the usual picaresque rogue, being guilty of murder, torture, rape and intolerant racism although the ultimate irony is that he is probably himself a Jew – a Jewish anti-Semite.

Pyat's beliefs are firmly rooted in the ideal of Plato's Republic, with its specific components and strict order, symbolised more specifically by the Byzantine Empire which in his view brought order to the world with its utopian vision of law, authority and nationalism. The problem with Plato's 'utopia' is that there was no room for poetry and creativity, hence no fantasy, amidst its militant sexism. Pyat's obsessive fear is that Islam and Judaism will bring chaos upon the western world and this xenophobia is aimed at the cities of Carthage and Jerusalem and what they represent mythologically and politically.

The four cities in the titles are significant. Byzantium (now Istanbul) became a powerful force under the control of Alexander the Great and in the 2nd century BC its army supported Rome in its various wars becoming, in effect, the Eastern wing of the Roman Empire. Eventually, in 330 AD Constantine the Great rebuilt the city as a new imperial capital renaming it Constantinople and it remained one of the richest cities in Christendom. After the schism of 1054, the Orthodox Church achieved independence from the Pope and developed its own sacraments, doctrine and rituals with which Pyat closely identifies however insincere his faith might be.

Carthage in North Africa probably began trading as early as the 9th century BC. The dominant religion involved human sacrifice to gods such as Baal, and therefore considered by Christians to be pagan, or worse, satanic. In ancient history Carthage forged a respectable empire led by such as Hannibal, but was eventually defeated by the more powerful Roman Empire after which it became a centre of Christianity. The city continued to change hands and in the 6th century it became part of the Byzantine Empire until it was seized by Arabs.

Jerusalem became the focus of the Crusades whereby European Christians fought Muslims for control of the Holy Land. Still tormented by political conflict Jerusalem is a holy site for Christians, Jews and Muslims and although Palestine was the birth land of Christ, it is interesting that the most important Christian power resides in Rome.

The so-called 'Eternal City', Rome was the capital of the greatest empire in ancient Europe. After Julius Caesar's death Augustus brought the republic to an end and appointed himself the first Emperor, forging a force of law and order on a world scale. Rome contains the Vatican state, home of the Roman Catholic Church, which boasts more than 900 million followers and as a city it most emphatically symbolises power and order.

Moorcock is keen to bring the reader's attention to the death of Empires, and by evoking these historically important cities manages to provide a metaphor for the ebb and flow of invasion, and the changing patterns of dominance between different cultures, religions and belief-systems. Byzantium is the Greek city of order and high art; Carthage is the domain of the pagan oriental. Jerusalem is the home of the Jew, whilst Rome is now the archetype of a fallen, decadent city that once ruled the world. Most of all, these picaresque novels are about a fluctuating period in European history, a time that caused confusion, change, violence and loss; appropriate subjects for fantasy.

In *Byzantium Endures*, we are confronted with Pyat's narration and let into the secrets of his strange childhood and upbringing. As an ambitious and pretentious adolescent, Pyat is guilty of arrogance, for if we are to believe even some of his claims, then he is certainly unusually gifted and somewhat unlucky not to have gained fame and public recognition. But the reader is always made to feel suspicious and wary of his arrogance as he tends to promote himself with extreme egomania – "I felt somewhat godlike … a messiah." This self-indulgent ranting leads to one of the first of his lengthy tirades in which he rewrites history and mythology, working himself into a frenzy. Because he cannot reconcile his anti-Semitism with his slightly deluded Christian faith he has had to recreate Jesus as a Greek, a prophet in the mould of Plato. "What can save the world? Not the Jewish-Moslem God … Only the Son can save us. Christ is a Greek." He stands firm in the belief that the spirit of the Roman Empire will continue in Russia as long as the nation does not lose faith in the great traditions and the ancient wisdom. Pyat depends upon the authority of such institutional traditions; he needs them to make sense of his own life and to retain a personal identity. The two world wars caused so much change and confusion that the individuals caught up in the chaos depended upon structures and rules to give their lives shape. In Moorcock's multiverse this eternal champion is an agent of Law fighting against liberalism, although it is ironic that his adolescence is a series of adventures involving illicit sex, smuggling, cocaine and masturbation. Pyat is also a victim of self-deception and the reader begins to lose faith in his perspective.

For Pyat, love is linked to tragedy. His childhood sweetheart Esme is in love with him, but he is too ignorant and full of his own self-importance to appreciate her love. Whilst he sleeps with prostitutes and lives a debauched life she waits patiently for him, and then years later when he comes to realise he has feelings for her it is too late as she has gone to help in the war as a nurse. Determined to find her he finally stumbles upon her as a pitiful and dirty prostitute, who tells him indifferently, "I've been raped so often I've got calluses on my cunt." This horrific memory continues to haunt him through all four books becoming a leitmotif for the entropy of romance and sexuality.

Esme personifies Russia in terms of innocence raped – a noble country wrecked by a civil conflict of sectarian warfare and continuing with this metaphor, Pyat then performs his greatest illusion so far. Being fickle, he is filled with hatred for Esme, accusing her of betrayal and shame for his home, so with a sleight of hand he reinvents both. He renames Kiev, 'the Rome of Russia' and then disappears to Constantinople/Byzantium which quickly becomes his true spiritual home ('Tsargrad'), just as later Hollywood becomes his new 'birthplace'.

Esme's reinvention is his greatest act of self-deception. By the second novel *The Laughter of Carthage*, he resolves to forget that the real Esme exists and with a Frankensteinian bravura creates a new Esme who will not betray him. The new 'Esme' is in fact a thirteen-year-old Romanian whore and to a Western reader this is little more than paedophilia. Unaware of his hypocrisy he even admits to himself, "Oh, Esme my sister … I never wanted you to be a woman." As soon as he can he sails to the USA and lies to his new Esme, promising to send for her but instead he satisfies his lusts in brothels and extends his hypocrisy to the extreme. "I remained loyal in spirit to Esme … (It was at a bawdyhouse, however, I had my first experience of a full-blooded Negress)." This is charged with extra irony, as he makes no secret of his vociferous racism. So still taking cocaine and acting the libertine, Pyat believes in his own innocence and importance.

The USA brings new optimism and a new identity, that of 'Max Peters', but even his faith in the Ku Klux Klan who preach white Protestant supremacy cannot provide the blueprint for the new Byzantium and inevitably he is betrayed by them and once again rejected. Before the second novel ends the holocaust is anticipated before the final testimony of Pyat, allowing Moorcock to compare the techniques of the Ku Klux Klan who "staple testicles to a tree", with those of Auschwitz Nazis who "passed their leisure skinning youths alive." Not allowing despondency to set in Pyat, now Max Peters, idealises Los Angeles before he has got there because after all – "The holy wood is where Parsifal discovered the Grail." It is difficult not to admire his optimism.

Jerusalem Commands is stark in its portrayal of evil, with Pyat becoming a more obvious victim and the most incredible thing about his story is that he survives so many horrors. Pyat in this sense represents us all as a survivor of this century who has witnessed some of the worst atrocities committed against the human race. This third volume compels the reader to become less judgmental of Pyat whose message has become sobering and challenging. His most noble comment comes at a successful time for him and is perhaps the moral of the whole sequence: "Now I have learned that Chaos is God's creation and it is our duty merely to order our part of the universe. Perhaps we are all too slow to accept responsibility. I cannot blame the British Empire, nor the American, nor Hitler, nor Mussolini, without accepting some blame myself." This jolts the reader from any comfortable distance or moral high ground for there is no place left at which to deflect our self-responsibility.

As the memoirs move towards the Nazi concentration camps, the mood grows stark and the atmosphere increasingly stifling. Pyat's visions become apocalyptic and demonic after he agrees to commit a real rape for a movie they are filming out in Egypt, and the memories become mingled in a haze of hallucinations in which he seems to enter the Egyptian underworld. These nightmares become, in turn, confused with the Nazi vision for 'Order, Security, Strength' and we are shown a glimpse into the horrors of the concentration camp, Sachsenhausen. Pyat, still arrogant, mistakes himself for Osiris who has been buried alive by Set, the lord of darkness, also known as Satan. During his death-like experience he is sexually abused and humiliated by a demoniac hermaphrodite: now the aggressor becomes the victim. This time the hermaphrodite is not a symbol of fulfilment, but rather of grotesque brutality at its most repulsive. This episode is written as a montage of dream, memory and myth and it is only when resurrected by Anubis that he escapes the horrors of this century. Moorcock warns us that we need beliefs and ideals to help us to make sense of the chaos; we need visions and ambitions to continue into the future, and we carry within us the spirit of ancestors and generations past.

Pyat is clearly not an anarchist, but Moorcock is, and by presenting reality from a distasteful perspective he makes a strong case against the rise of political authority and tyrannical forms of control. Moorcock stated his views on power in a letter to *The London Review of Books*: "I'd guess that roughly the same proportions of sadists and psychopaths, useful for genocidal work, exists in any society and emerges at appropriate times. It's apparently impossible for an ordinary middle-class person to imagine the deep lust for power at any price, the violent sexualised fantasies and ambitions of that frustrated sadist who could very easily be a neighbour, a colleague or even a spouse. Most of us would prefer to think such people exceptional. Or fictional. Or foreign. I believe they represent a fairly large percentage of the world's population."

The "Between the Wars" sequence attempts to portray the various struggles for power on both global and individual platforms and Moorcock interrogates such uprisings in history, seeking to highlight and understand forms of cruelty and horror. In Pyat's commentary the reader is allowed an insight into an individual's struggle for internal sanity. It is in these "historical" novels that Moorcock brings the fantasy of his earlier sword and sorcery novels up to date for just like the fantasy novels, we see a world in constant conflict – the struggle for power whilst cities and races rise and fall as a symbol of the flux in human social order.

8: Von Bek

The von Bek family have become important in Moorcock's later writing, allowing him to connect books and series by the use of names that constantly reappear, once again allowing him to play tricks with characters, settings and situations. Much of his recent output follows various members of the von Bek family. In 1992 Moorcock anthologised the two von Bek novels, *The War Hound and the World's Pain* and *The City in the Autumn Stars* as the first volume in the Millennium Orion Eternal Champion series. Also added is an early but revised story, 'The Pleasure Garden of Felipe Sagittarius', which is only related because the author changed the name of the narrator from Minos Aquilinas to Minos von Bek and Moorcock continues to play with names in many of his novels and short stories. For example, the recent short story anthology, *London Bone* (2001), abounds with various von Beks and its anglicised form, Begg. *Tales From the Texas Woods* (1997) includes a detective story in which the famous Sexton Blake has become Sexton Begg, thus even relating him to the von Bek clan. The link with the Eternal champion is made explicit in *The Dreamthief's Daughter* (2001), presenting Ulrich von Bek as Elric's doppelganger and von Bek is also the protagonist of another important novel, *The Brothel In Rosenstrasse* (1982).

However, Ulrich von Bek first appeared in print in 1981 in *The War Hound and the World's Pain,* which was runner up for the World Fantasy Award. This literary fantasy utilises the structures and themes of Romantic literature, borrowing its mood and atmosphere from Gothic fiction. It offers a post-modern inversion of one of the main Christian myths (or at least Milton's interpretation as set out in *Paradise Lost*), being an apocalyptic vision of the completion of the cycle of creation and redemption in which Lucifer yearns for his own return to Heaven. Satan becomes the most sympathetic character in the book, full of remorse having grown weary of his struggle to fulfil his duty as enemy of the world. He hopes that his genuine penitence will lead him to his eventual atonement.

He is a tragic figure – a victim of hubris – fatigued by his role as tempter, now a figure of noble pathos. "He bore an aura about His person, which I had never associated with the Devil: perhaps it was a kind of dignified humility combined with an almost limitless power." For Moorcock, Lucifer is now more human-like in his frailty, filled with guilt and sorrow, looking through "melancholy, terrible eyes" and speaking with "exquisite sadness", telling the protagonist, Ulrich von Bek, how he yearns to be reconciled with God. Satan has become a Byronic figure.

Lucifer takes von Bek on a guided tour of Hell, which, surprisingly, is a cold and hopeless place, unlike Dante's *Inferno,* where Satan roams bored but worried that he may have misunderstood God's original commission. The novel becomes an inversion of the Faustian myth, where von Bek can gain life and rescue his soul from damnation if he can find the Holy Grail whose restoration will lead to a "cure for the world's pain".

Moorcock is not so interested in Christian, moralistic symbolism, but he uses the grail to portray a romantic notion of love. Von Bek, like Elric for Cymoril, is spurred on by his love for the mysterious and beautiful Sabrina, a servant of Lucifer. Love is a frequent source of energy in Moorcock's work and is the only cure for entropy, the inevitable, slow death of the universe. In Moorcock's work, the grail can also be a person or a place, and is usually the key to manipulating the time streams of the multiverse.

The reader is forced to revise set assumptions regarding good and evil, now in the guise of law and chaos. The most evil character in the novel is not Lucifer but Klosterheim, ironically a knight of Christ. Klosterheim symbolises the corruption and bloodlust of the early church, most apparent in the Holy Inquisition, another Gothic context. Moorcock is presenting the church as an institution of order and control and, more controversially, Satan is no longer evil.

Eventually, von Bek stumbles upon the Grail, a simple clay cup and is told that "the cure is within every one of us", for each individual is responsible for his own balance and harmony, particularly the balance between reason and sensibility. Von Bek's quest was really to discover freedom from divine powers and fate and this inevitably leads to cosmic irony. Rather than rely on religion, von Bek's quest is to discover his own identity and he learns that "one must not seek to become a saint or sinner, God or Devil. One must seek to become human and to love the fact of one's humanity." The cure for the world's pain lies in your own self-belief.

The sequel, *The City in the Autumn Stars* (1986), follows the destiny of humanity from an age of superstition to the Age of Reason and the beginning of Industrialisation. Claiming to be the picaresque confessions of Manfred von Bek and set in 1794, we meet von Bek on his return from revolutionary Paris, who, like his friend, Tom Paine, had become disillusioned with Robespierre and the Jacobins, eventually denouncing the despotism of the blood-thirsty mob. Bored with politics, von Bek decides to become a hedonist and follow his family motto, "Do you the Devil's work."

Moorcock, it seems, is still unhappy with the final version of the novel after being told by his editor to cut out a third of the original manuscript delivered to him and the author has admitted that it is "a book with only a little backbone left." He has expressed a certain embarrassment about the book's failings, but it is probably better than he imagines. The bombastic language and symbolism are, at times, contrived or ambiguous, but they only add to the novel's poetic and dream-like quality. The overarching themes are that of gender identity and the development of rationality over religion, using the symbolism of alchemy as the transition between magic and science. Whilst the book begins with a strong historical setting, it quickly moves off to the fantasy realm of Mittelmarch via Moorcock's beloved Mirenburg, the perfect city. Stylistically, the novel shifts between comedy of manners and gothic fantasy.

Von Bek is pursued by two sinister knights, Montsorbier and Klosterheim, who also appeared in *The Warhound and the World's Pain*, and his flight seems pointless until he meets Libussa, the Countess of Crete, who he pursues after falling in love with her. His companion is the ever cheerful Scotsman known as St. Odhran, a student of the Montgolfier brothers and owner of his own hot air balloon in which they make their frequent escapes. It is when he flies in the balloon that von Bek realises the potential power provided by these miracles of technology: "my ascent ... by aerial ship was the first moment I truly realised the world had embarked upon a radical new course in which mankind's theories and dreams could now be made reality." Reason, or law, begins its ascendancy over Romance, or chaos.

In his nightmares, von Bek has vivid hallucinations in which classical mythology becomes confused with alchemical symbolism, always leading him to the image of the hermaphrodite, the ideal union of the male and female. The visions continue to haunt von Bek to the end. When he finally confronts Libussa he has become so obsessed with his idealised love for her that he allows her to control him and he takes the passive, or traditionally feminine role in their relationship, symbolised by mercury. Libussa takes the active, male part, symbolised by bronze or sulphur and these elements are signs of sexual chemistry. It transpires that she is an alchemist waiting for the Astral Concordance that occurs every thousand years, when different worlds intersect to "offer harmony, a cure for the world's pain." This ability to cure all diseases is also the main property of the elusive philosopher's stone sought by all alchemists. Her search for balance in the struggle between reason and the supernatural is to be discovered in the conjoining at this time of male and female in the creation of a hermaphrodite. Libussa reassures von Bek that "the sum of the two of us would be god-like."

Being a von Bek, he soon finds himself searching for the Holy Grail, meeting on the way the delightful Lord Renyard, the fox king of rogues, who reads Voltaire but suffers from ennui, and the more mysterious Goat Queen. He also witnesses a satanic cult sacrificing a ritual lamb, but learns through a meeting with Lucifer himself that these so-called devil worshippers have nothing to do with him and that even Klosterheim and Montsorbier serve only their own selfish ends.

Lucifer gives von Bek the sword of Paracelsus, a sixteenth century alchemist of our own world, who sought the secret elixir or philosopher's stone that would restore the celestial harmony between the human body and the stars – a cure for the world's pain. His sword was said to contain the devil, which gives a neat parallel with Elric's sword Stormbringer. It was also believed by some that Paracelsus successfully created the artificial man known as the 'homunculus', an obsession later shared by famous English occultist Aleister Crowley, as depicted in his novel, *Moonchild* (1929). The homunculus is the alchemist's attempt to create a messiah or superman through the use of arcane magic, secret tinctures and occult 'science'.

In *The City in the Autumn Stars*, Libussa is preparing von Bek as her partner in a ritual marriage of sulphur and mercury to create harmony and a new messiah, who will be immortal and omnipotent. This hermaphrodite will be "A leader who no longer spreads the word of God, but spreads the word of humanity", announcing a new era of science and knowledge finally defeating religion and superstition. Although the experiment is essentially a failure, von Bek, ironically, learns a great deal about humanity and love. Whilst he has become obsessed with his love for Libussa, her affections for him were seemingly insincere as she only served her own purposes, mainly her search for self-empowerment. Ultimately she is guilty of hubris by believing she can control nature itself. The Grail, symbolic perhaps of love or even God, who remains strangely absent throughout, will not allow the power of the Beast to rule.

The apocalyptic ending is somewhat confusing, but that is in the essence of alchemy to be hermetic and obscure, and so Moorcock brings in arcane symbolism, such as the eagle, which seems to represent Lucifer himself who cannot be controlled by mere humans. Von Bek is also confused and believes, wrongly, that he has betrayed the woman he loves.

Although he loses Libussa she continues to live in his memory and desire, for he seems to have discovered the true meaning of love. Whilst she was using him for her own ends he had quietly confided in her, making the most poignant statement in the book, by telling her, "I love you for who you are. I love you as a human creature." And so humanity wins and even Lucifer realises that the world is the realm of men and women now. Fate lies in our hands.

Many of Moorcock's more recent short stories develop similar themes and ideas, most notably in the important story 'The Clapham Antichrist' (originally appearing as 'Lunching with the Antichrist' in 1993). This key story develops the von Bek family history and links Edwin Begg with the Rose, who together have a hermaphroditic child who becomes a messiah leading the world into a new stage in evolution. Similarly, in 'The Cairene Purse' (1990) we learn how Beatrice von Bek falls in love with a hermaphrodite alien and then gives birth to a messiah who dies. These stories are certainly related to *The City in the Autumn Stars.*

Moorcock's original intention was to write a trilogy as he explained recently on the internet in his question and answer website. "I originally intended to do three novels – one set in the Age of Religion, as it were, one in the Age of Reason and one in Nazi times, so while the Elric (*The Dreamthief's Daughter*) is the first book in a new series, it's also the last in another!" The third book in the trilogy was abandoned and became the new Elric novel.

Moorcock and his publishers, Earthlight, caused great excitement with the announcement of this new Elric book in 2001 and *The Dreamthief's Daughter* is the first of a new trilogy also linked to the generic name von Bek. Narrated in first person by Ulric von Bek, an albino living in 1930s Germany, his life becomes entwined with his doppelgänger – a certain albino demi-god called Elric of Melniboné. Before uniting with his alter-ego, von Bek dreams of flying on the back of a dragon and tells of his black sword, Ravenbrand. In the first section of the novel the reader gets the German perspective of internal politics and events leading up to the Second World War, explaining how Hitler was seen as a strong leader who would "bring us stability." Von Bek, however, quickly sees the error in his nation's judgement and swears to destroy Hitler. He sees that this stability or obsession for order is far too simplistic and he bemoans the folly of his countrymen who failed to understand that, "human beings are far more complex than simple truth and simple truth is fine for argument and clarification, but it is not an instrument for government." Although we only meet Hess as a character within the narrative, succinct comments are made about the main Nazi protagonists. According to reliable accounts, Hitler was 'boring', Himmler was 'a prude', Goerring was a 'snob', Goebbels was 'withdrawn' and Hess was a 'vegetarian crank'.

Later von Bek revises his opinion of the Führer describing him as "deeply banal and profoundly mad." He knows that the Nazi salute is a poor copy of the Roman salute used in the film *Quo Vadis*, and in the end he almost pities Hitler for being a small man out of his depth.

Ulric von Bek is visited by two characters from Moorcock's roll-call, Prince Gaynor and Klosterheim, who demand that von Bek hand over his sword, Ravenbrand. Prince Gaynor, Corum's old adversary, was introduced in *The Queen of the Swords* and reappeared against Elric in *The Revenge of the Rose* whilst the sinister figure of Klosterheim continues to be von Bek's eternal adversary. Their appearance in *The Dreamthief's Daughter* begins a supernatural adventure, as we learn that Gaynor is merely using the Nazi uniform to tap into a greater and more ancient power. Hitler's rise to power is only a microcosm or an echo of a larger story being played out on many planes concurrently. Von Bek gets caught up in a nightmarish chase through the mythical land of Mittelmarch, the borderlands between the human world and Faerie; a place similar to the Nordic alfheim, or Elfland. Moorcock previously used the Middlemarch as a location in *The City In the Autumn Stars*.

Professor of English David Punter remarks in his book on Gothic fantasy, *The Literature of Terror, Volume 2,* how "Moorcock especially demonstrates a considerable power in the manipulation of mythic and quasi-mythic materials", and in *The Dreamthief's Daughter,* the author startlingly and successfully manipulates ancient Egyptian, Celtic, Arthurian and Teutonic mythologies into a story of Wagnerian proportions that intertwines with Moorcock's own multiverse of Tanelorn and the Eternal Champion, creating a contemporary myth.

In 1930s Germany, von Bek is taken to Sachsenhausen prison camp where his brutal torture is described with a distant and indifferent voice. Von Bek's dispassionate narration adds to the general horror the reader already feels towards the Nazis and their abuse of power. Eventually, of course, the reliable League of Temporal Adventurers, including the ubiquitous Oswald Bastable, help von Bek to escape and divert him towards his fate of fighting for the balance.

It transpires that von Bek is a version of Elric in a parallel world, and through the dreams that have been directed by Oona, the dreamthief's daughter, the two champions merge to become "two men in a single body" for about seventy pages of the novel. It seems that dreams are merely glimpses of these other lives and balance is restored when we move between these lives and change them. The true plot then unravels as the eternal champion fights with Gaynor the Damned; chaos against law.

Once again, Moorcock plays with names and in a moment of post-modern satire he calls one of the decrepit, insane goddesses of law Duchess Miggea, an anagram of Maggie (Thatcher) and one of the ineffective knights with a wide grin is named Baron Blare. Moonglum, the eternal companion reappears and one cannot help but wonder if Oona is a version of Una Persson, who is often the companion of Oswald Bastable. Links are frequently made to the connected novel, *The Fortress Of the Pearl,* in which Elric meets Oona's mother.

The Dreamthief's Daughter becomes a quest for the elusive and inconstant Holy Grail, which we are told can transform into any object, such as a sword or even a person. The champions then travel the unpredictable moonbeam roads to find a realm known as 'the Grey Fees', which are made up of "the fundamental stuff of the multiverse", the life force itself created by human memory and desire: as if imagination and will could become matter itself. 'Grey Fees', we are told, is actually a corruption of Grail Fields and thus the quest comes full circle as Elric and von Bek attempt to stop Gaynor from becoming a new and corrupt god. Power, in many of Moorcock's novels, is symbolised by a talisman and his favourite is that of the Arthurian legend. The Holy Grail was originally the chalice from which Christ drank at the last supper and for Moorcock it comes to represent the Balance itself. Power also resides in swords, coming from another Arthurian legend – that of Excalibur. Charlemagne had his sword and Roland blew his horn known as Olivant, and so Moorcock, like so many fantasists, employs symbols to represent supernatural and archaic power.

The novel's grand finale gives a new twist to the Battle of Britain and echoes the typical Moorcockian climax on the scale of Götterdämmerung. Normality is restored and von Bek is left to evaluate the effect not only on his homeland but on the entire multiverse. However, at the end of the novel he has still not found the grail or his lost son.

The Dreamthief's Daughter leaves the reader with a challenging remark about our own British culture in the 21st Century, as von Bek assesses the state of England, once great with its poets and historians, but now decadent and in entropy, "because she no longer possessed men of such integrity and breadth of vision." The task of the Eternal Champion is to rise above the general malaise and apathy of our lazy culture and to make a real difference in the lives that we lead and the actions that we choose to take. In the words of von Bek – "It seemed we were all fated to live identical lives in billions of counter-realities rarely able to change our stories yet constantly striving to do so. Occasionally one of us was successful." Although Elric has become a demi-god, a warrior who rescues humanity from the grip of evil, what *The Dreamthief's Daughter* really demonstrates is that the true champions are "the invisible people" – the normal men and women of our own world and time, or as Oswald Bastable explains to von Bek: "The ordinary heroes and heroines of these appalling conflicts between corrupted Chaos and degenerate Law." Perhaps we are all avatars of the Eternal Champion, needing to understand our own fate to enable us to fight for the balance within our own individual lives and for society

Another novel about the ubiquitous von Beks that requires brief discussion here, is *The Brothel In Rosenstrasse* (1982), which examines similar themes of Europe in conflict, this time at the end of the nineteenth century; the *fin de siècle*. Moorcock sets the novel in Mirenburg, the capital of Wäldenstein – a location so realistic that it gets readers reaching for their atlases. Mirenburg is on the brink of a civil war, threatened with destruction as the novel's protagonist, Count von Bek, muses that "Man's greatest monuments, his architecture, never outlast his acts of aggression."

The Brothel In Rosenstrasse begins with a history of Mirenburg, an idealised Bohemia, giving the novel its vivid identity and sense of place. It seems Mirenburg owes something to such cities as Prague and Vienna and it again becomes the setting for *The City In the Autumn Stars* at the end of the eighteenth century. Mirenburg is probably also a version of Tanelorn, the resting place of the Eternal Champion.

The second part of *The Brothel In Rosenstrasse* details the sexual appetite within the brothel amongst its upper class patrons, who in the third part are disturbed by the political upheaval brought about by revolutionary terrorism. This intense novel details the decadent lives of the prosperous classes in the decadent setting of Frau Schmetterling's brothel, which comes to symbolise an old world order of sensuality and epicureanism. The eroticism retains a dignity and is described with a sense of aesthetic taste by the voice of a connoisseur, exposing Moorcock's own familiarity with brothels. In fact, sexuality becomes a political metaphor for the changing power in Eastern Europe: sex is more important than love and old von Bek and his sixteen year old lover can never be compatible. The protagonist, Count von Bek is selfish and unsympathetic throughout. The brothel itself is a microcosm of elegance, like Mirenburg itself: gothic and subject to ancient laws. Neither, however, can stand up to the violence of modern warfare. The self-indulgence of the powerful classes spoils the intimacy of relationships, illuminating how greed and selfishness, like war, are destructive not only to individuals but whole societies.

9: LONDON

The symphonic novel *Mother London* (1988) is a celebration of
Moorcock's home. It explores the history of the twentieth century and
expresses the individual anxiety and struggle for identity within the
modern city. But mostly, it is about London herself – and London is
the protagonist of the novel. As the author states, "London – thanks in
a large part to her writers – has always been the richest, most coherent,
civilised, tolerant and inspiring cosmopolitan megapolis in the world."
Mother London is an epic project, masterfully executed and, according
to the author, his magnum opus and many critics agreed. The late
novelist, Angela Carter reviewed Moorcock's book in The Guardian
with great enthusiasm, praising it as "a vast, uncorseted, sentimental,
comic, elegiac salmagundi of a novel", whilst American reviewer Paul
Witcover hailed it as "an authentic work of genius." *Mother London*
was shortlisted for the Whitbread Prize.

Moorcock evokes 'place' in his novels with some eloquence. He
created the decadent city of Mirenburg in *The Brothel in Rosenstrasse*
and Gloriana's Albion remains his elegy to the historical London, but in
Mother London he celebrates the modern city, which has become a
sentient, conscious character. Moorcock's London becomes more than a
single place, but contains a complete realm of mythology – a multiverse.

The iconicity of the city is of particular interest and as an icon the city fulfils many functions: such as that of the labyrinth with its dark secrets; as mother protecting her offspring; as a destructive asylum of anxiety and control; and finally, as a living creature. The people and the city are symbiotic, for there is no city without inhabitants and those who live there are shaped by the place. London is a mother, but not necessarily a benevolent one and she speaks through the pain and passion of her children, like a Greek Chorus. This is a good example of a polyphonic novel, which narrates using a number of different voices, perspectives or viewpoints.

Mother London follows a complex structure that is a non-chronological pattern which undulates like a tide to and fro, forwards and backwards, framed by vignettes of the main characters set in the present. Unusually, the climax occurs in the middle with horrific descriptions of the Blitz, which leaves a gradual and anti-climactic ending. Motifs are developed and themes are revisited throughout the novel and this non-linear and seemingly random collage makes it a surreal picture of London and its history. The landscape and inhabitants of the city are explored through an episodic narrative carefully placed around the chorus of the city's collective consciousness.

Moorcock allows us three narrative perspectives, each of which is a facet of himself; David, Josef and Mary, who are three outpatients at the same psychiatric clinic. The most clearly autobiographical chapters are those narrated in first person by David Mummery, a carefully chosen name referring to the medieval folk performer, the mummer, and implying a hypocritical or theatrical display. His first name has a religious significance and connection with Christ, often called the Son of David (he is taken to Bethlehem Mental Hospital) completing the trinity of Mary (a resurrected spirit and mother) and Josef (a father figure).

Mummery describes himself as an urban anthropologist, a role also being undertaken by Moorcock in the writing of this novel. The narrative complexity can be seen in Jungian terms whereby Moorcock's ego/self is divided into three main archetypes or masks: Mummery is the child, symbolising the whole self; Mary is the anima and Josef is both the wise man and the fool. Each facet of the author also reflects an interest: Mummery's perspective is autobiographical and of a personal London; Josef stands for a nostalgic London and represents the life force of the indigenous Londoner; Mary lives in the dreamworld of a mythological London. All three Londons are real and they overlap.

The most enigmatic character is David Mummery who represents the young Moorcock. *Mother London* is an introverted and personal novel containing streams of consciousness and mystic vision. Other than *Letters From Hollywood*, Moorcock's attempts at autobiography have been fictionalised and unreliable and Moorcock openly admits that Glogauer, Elric and Jerry Cornelius represent aspects of himself. Mummery is likewise self-deprecating and infernally melancholic, brooding and self-indulgent, a familiar trait of both Elric and Cornelius.

One of Moorcock's earliest memories was watching the Blitz over South London just as described by David Mummery, and the war-torn ruins became a childhood playground. In an interview Moorcock described this epiphanal childhood experience: "I grew up in a constantly altered landscape ... but it wasn't frightening to children of my age. There was an enormous amount of freedom involved." Like Mummery, Moorcock was also expelled from an experimental school in East Sussex, he really did have an uncle who was a civil servant living at 10 Downing Street and he played in a skiffle band called The Greenhorns in 1957.

A chapter that stands out for its social commentary and linked directly to Moorcock's own experience is one narrated by Mummery which describes the police brutality and racism at the Notting Hill Carnival in 1977. The narrator witnesses riots and has inside information that the police and 'white residents' had formulated a plan to start a riot so that future carnivals would be banned. This frightening account concurs with Moorcock's account in his political tract *The Retreat From Liberty* (1983), a discussion of the erosion of civil rights in contemporary Britain. In this political polemic he describes another moment during the carnival, which later became a scene in *Mother London*: "at one point a friend sat in a predominantly black café while a line of policemen banged their truncheons on their riot shields by way of challenge. Inside, he said, everyone kept their cool and ignored the police ... The blacks maintained their apparent insouciance while the natives outside tried to break their nerves with displays of aggression."

Notting Hill Gate in the 1960-70s was an eclectic, decadent and mystical environment full of folklore and conflict and there is no doubt that living there heavily affected Moorcock's personal and political outlook. His warning conclusion in *The Retreat from Liberty* is one that is explored by much of his fiction: "Whether we are destroyed by a process of social collapse or by the explosion of nuclear missiles the fault will lie ultimately with us – in our own capacity for self-deception and our unwillingness to deal directly and courageously with the realities and injustices of our daily lives."

Josef represents a more mature Moorcock – suave and romantic. Like David and Mary he is a psychiatric patient who can hear voices, using his telepathic skill in the war to rescue trapped victims. He is a hero managing to seduce, save lives and converse with a demon, but we also witness him visiting a prostitute and making a drunken, naked spectacle of himself. He is a Falstaffian anti-hero who in an inspired moment of naive insanity manages to miraculously defuse a bomb and save lives. The description is closer to Don Quixote than Achilles: "With a gasp, almost a sob, he rammed the shears into the works and snipped. He snipped twice more, trusting to whatever instincts he had ... then snipped again as the bile rose in his mouth and he felt he would drown in it ... It grumbled, whimpered and grew silent." Josef attempts to find his own personal balance between the chaos of his psychic powers and his own order. For him "His routine and his own particular medicine are his protection against a chaos." Josef faces physical and mental chaos and manages to survive what Moorcock implies were two of the most destructive forces of the twentieth century – World War II and Thatcherism.

The decades present us with changing cultures. The fifties are austere, the sixties exciting and avant-garde, but the seventies see the beginning of entropy. Moorcock frequently celebrates the sixties, but like many since, now realises this romantic view is a somewhat unreal one.

Moorcock continues to comment on British culture through other characters, many of whom show cynical reactions to the so-called hippy revolution. For example, Patsy Meakin, a minor character, and avant-garde filmmaker uses the spirit of the age to his own advantage: "The counter-culture had taken Patsy by surprise and only received his interest because of the pretty girls it attracted ... If it promised the joys of teenage dolly birds, good drugs, and the chance of an orgy or two, he was willing to look a bit of a twit." Moorcock suggests this may have been a prevalent view.

Josef blames what he calls the 'Thatcher-belt' for ruining the real London. "You hear them moaning about the people who were born there as if those were the interlopers! It's classic imperialism." Josef's fear is that London will become a theme park, such as Dickensland and this fear is realised when David's cousin George outlines his plans to open The New Ludgate Chop House on the site of The Old King Lud pub. Ludd was the founder and protector of London, a Celtic god of great importance to history, myth and fantasy, and it seems quite ludicrous that he becomes the icon for a plastic theme-restaurant. Mary sees this as an inevitable process of the self-mythologisation of civilisation, but Josef rejects such farcical deception.

The Scaramanga sisters, whom Josef saves, represent the more rural, nostalgic, village life, which has been swallowed up by Greater London. They live in a cottage by the canal with barges at the end of the garden and drink tea from china cups, but their haven is ruined by the Blitz: "All the insects, all the butterflies and birds were gone, as in a fairy tale." It is as if something beautiful has been destroyed; London, like some Garden of Eden, has been spoiled by man's pride and greed.

Josef's visions are the most vivid. During the Blitz he witnesses an apocalyptic hallucination of the city coming to life rousing "the sleeping gods of London" like some modern day Blake. These sequences are the most obvious moments of fantasy in which the three aspects of the city combine. He sees angels and giants from the city's mythology, and hears the voices of all the inhabitants and is aware of "his voice joining the millions to form a single monumental howl." As in Moorcock's early sword and sorcery novels, angels and demons continue to symbolise a more personal battle and that internal conflict is projected onto the larger canvasses of world politics and even heaven and hell. After the war Josef continues having supernatural experiences, which he relates as normal events – "I was walking there … when I ran slap into a demon." Josef's vision during the Blitz reads like a description of the hordes of chaos in one of the author's earlier fantasies.

Mary is a more ambiguous character whose grasp on reality is incomplete as she remains in her dream world comprised of

Hollywood glamour and surreal fantasy. Mary, like London, is a mother who has survived the war, but has trouble coping with the modern world. Having woken from her coma she hears voices and seems to have second sight, but the voices are often brutal and pornographic and she therefore tries to block them out.

It is during 1970 that Mary, Josef and David find the greatest fulfilment. It is a moment of perfect happiness in a fairground on a merry-go-round. All the characters agree "they would gladly live this instant forever." Acid has enabled some kind of mystical 'multiversal vision' and the colour and wonder of the fairground is augmented by the gathering hippies, crowded as if at the Isle of Wight Festival: "in afghans and bell-bottoms and flowers they call themselves the children of the sun." In contrast to Josef's demonic vision, this is a glimpse of paradise and a utopian end time. Back in 1975 Moorcock and his band The Deep Fix released their recording *New Worlds Fair*, a concept album about a fairground which becomes the last place in a world which is dissipating. Songs such as 'Last Merry Go Round' and 'Dodgem Dude' follow the dangerous rides and false dreams. The fairground is a sinister place where customers experience both pleasure and fear, and become lost in a fake haze of movement, smells and sensuality. It is an ersatz world, full of corruption and profit, in which the rust is covered by a veneer of paint and the customer is hypnotised and momentarily beguiled. It is interesting that in *Mother London* the characters are happiest at this moment. All their problems are forgotten and each has become an innocent child distracted from all tragedy that has befallen. All their friends join them on the final ride, which seems to endlessly repeat itself. This moment of ecstasy is orgiastic, the jouissance unendingly repeated and from the merry-go-round, David cries a human and rather pathetic plea – "Don't let it ever stop." Perhaps escaping reality – fantasy itself – is the only answer.

The novel ends with the figure of Old Non, a wandering tramp, whose name is an anagram of London. She knows all the legends about Gog and Magog, the giants guarding London; about Bran the Celtic giant whose head is buried under Parliament Hill; of all the ghosts of the Bloody Tower; of Dick Turpin and Dan Leno. Moorcock's comforting, authorial voice reminds the reader of the value of fantasy. "By means of our myths and legends we maintain a sense of what we are worth and who we are. Without them we should undoubtedly go mad."

London, home to millions, is herself growing senile and is personified by the dotty, homeless storyteller, who wanders the streets, sharing her wisdom like the last surviving wyrd sister keeping alive the ancient mysteries and eternal wonders of the city. By giving one subtle reference, Moorcock completes his own multiverse by having Josef refer to Old Non at one point as 'Mrs C.' This has huge implications with regard to Moorcock's complicated internal referencing, because Mrs C is Jerry Cornelius' mother. It is difficult to discern the seriousness of Moorcock's intention; being unpredictable he may just be teasing readers or making an important statement. Mrs C certainly fulfils a universal role similar to London, and if Jerry is Everyman then there is no difficulty in following the argument that his coarse, senile but loveable mum, is in a multiversal sense, also the mother of us all. This may be the author's joke.

Even if London has failed to realise Blake's vision, then like Josef, we must cling to our hope that humanity is essentially good. This is Moorcock's Romantic notion. "London endures. Her stories endure. People's demand for Romance endures. And I retain confidence in human nature."

Just like Albion in *Gloriana*, London contains the 'inner landscapes' of memory, dreams and the 'collective unconscious.' The irony is that the protagonists are deemed 'mad', but as readers, we are shown that true madness comes with war, destroying all that is dear to us: our families, our identity, and our own home. *Mother London* is a complex novel about love, loss and redemption in which the city becomes a metaphor for faith and salvation. The real London is, of course, the one in your mind.

King of the City (2000) is again set in London, although there is less of a sense of the city as a sentient character and more explicit nostalgia, which cannot always be taken at face value. *King of the City* may well be more autobiographical and it certainly updates the history of London, which ended at 1985 in *Mother London*. Unlike its predecessor, *King of the City* escapes beyond the realm of London, trespassing on to foreign soils, including Rwanda and Kosovo; places in conflict at the time the novel was written.

The structure of the novel is once again unorthodox. The first half of the book describes vignettes of popular London life punctuated with anti-capitalist political polemics, and then a conventional plot only begins after the first 200 pages. Writer Ian Sinclair accurately described the novel as "a comprehensive encyclopedia of lost lives, uncelebrated loci, trashed cultural memory."

Its tone is decidedly existentialist set by the anti-conservative voice of the narrator, Dennis Dover, who pessimistically, sums up the twentieth century: "You start with the first concentration camps, an Imperial war, carving up Africa, add a chorus of all the agonised millions calling from the dirt of no man's land, into the Russian Civil War, the Chinese Civil War, the Spanish Civil War, Stalin, the rise of Fascism, the Holocaust, World War Two, Hiroshima, Korea, Vietnam, Cambodia, Afghanistan, Iraq and Bosnia, Rwanda and East Timor. And Kosovo of course … What a bloody century." When seen from this realistic perspective, Moorcock leaves the reader wondering exactly what we have learned from the lessons of history.

The first and last lines of the novel echo each other and emphasise the themes of 'myths and miracles', subjects familiar to all fantasy readers. However, this novel is set in a very real and recognisable present-day, with the first person narration using slang, expletives and street talk. Dennis, or Den, a 'paparazzo' photojournalist and rock star, is once more an aspect of Michael Moorcock himself, writer, traveller and leader of the band The Deep Fix. Den's early experience of playing guitar at a gig echoes Elric's wielding of the black blade, Stormbringer: "My Rickenbacker was bucking out of my control, screaming with complicated lusts, radiating funny black light. Its strings were silver rays piercing infinity. Roadways through the multiverse." He later plays a guitar called a Black Falcon that gives "the sense of you being the guitar and the guitar being you."

In fact, just like *Mother London*, there are three main characters, all of whom reflect a persona of the author. Den's foil is Rosie Beck, his cousin, with whom he is in love and who, like an aspect of the eternal champion, spends her life helping the victims of poverty, war and injustice.

Barbican Begg, a multi-millionaire, best represents the spirit of free enterprise against whom Rosie and Den are sworn to struggle, although their ways are, at times, dubious. ("If the City and Wall

Street acknowledged a holy trinity then it was God, Washington and Barbican Begg"). As the millionaire continues to ruin and destroy London herself, Den develops a deeper resentment, feeling that his "roots were being chopped off." Once again, Moorcock shows capitalism as the enemy of community and personal identity.

A recognisable character from Moorcock's cast of regular characters is Al Rikh, a mysterious but powerful albino sheikh. There are also a number of real people involved, such as Hawkwind singer and poet Robert Calvert, as well as most of the Hawkwind and Deep Fix members. For example, an important character in *King of the City* is Tubby Ollis, whose real name is Dorian Theakston, and the drummers listed on the two Deep Fix albums are D. Theaker and Terry Ollis (also of Hawkwind). Tubby is an agent of chaos fighting bigotry and politicians, or at least organising having custard pies thrown at them and Tubby's sub-plot with the defence of his mill is one of the most vivid episodes in the novel.

Den's discussion of British rock music is anecdotal and realistic, referring to names such as David Bowie, Alex Harvey, Annie Lennox and even claiming that, "The job in The Police was between me and Andy Summers." Later on, Den cringes at the thought that he was nearly in a band with Bill Clinton and Tony Blair. As *King of the City* develops, it becomes Moorcock's personal fantasy in which his alter-ego, Den, makes a come-back with Deep Fix and becomes "suddenly more famous than Michael Jackson." They appear on 'Top of the Pops', get a single banned on US radio and perform a gig on Tower Bridge before Princess Diana and an all-star audience, relayed by satellite television across the world.

Cynical about British politics and mainstream culture, Denny enjoys making sarcastic remarks about prime ministers 'Margaret Hatchet' and 'Tony Blurr' – "Mrs T used the language of liberal humanism to reinstall feudalism" – and like many he sees New Labour continuing the policies of Margaret Thatcher. In the latter part of the novel, he gets drawn into some of the horrors in Kosovo, experiencing personal tragedy that leads to suicidal paranoia. But it is through recognising the terrible and tragic mistakes of the twentieth century that mankind could finally learn the simple truth – "That common dream. That place of peace and good health we were promised as the prize of our progress." The only hope lies not in consumerism, capitalism or fascism, but in the ideals of what anarchist philosopher Peter Kropotkin called 'mutual aid.' Den comforts himself with a similar vision, "of a mutually respecting civil and civilised world, judging itself by its best ideas and actions."

He eventually gets a second chance to reinvent himself, find love and see the world through new eyes. Rosie's conspiracy has created a revolution that will make the world a better place and she is identified as the true eternal champion, or perhaps she is the controller of the balance who can manipulate people and history. Den is eventually king of a new city of hope and ideals, and this is the miracle – that London can once more become "the best and most progressive, the richest and greatest city the world has ever known." But happiness comes not with money and fame – that can only be found with love. The miracle of peace and justice may only be a myth, but never underestimate the power of myth and fantasy. Moorcock has developed his own multiversal myth further and his moral is optimistic – where would we be without the power to dream?

Michael Moorcock himself is the king of the multiverse or at least his London. (Publication for *King of the City* coincided with the election for London Mayor and the publicity posters announced, 'Vote for Michael Moorcock'). The entire novel is a celebratory monologue for the city that is his real home, and the author manipulates London just as Elric wields the symbiotic sword, Stormbringer. Even if Michael Moorcock now lives in Texas, his heart and soul must surely remain in London.

10: EXPANDING THE MULTIVERSE

Now resident in Texas, Moorcock continues to develop his ever-expanding multiverse. His triptych of novels known as 'The Second Ether' is not properly a trilogy although marketed as such. Like many of Moorcock's novels, they claim to be manuscripts written by someone else – in this case they are the property of Edwin Begg. *Blood* (1994) is an experimental novel compiled from previously published episodes. *Fabulous Harbours* (1995) is a collection of related stories about various Beks and Beggs, leaving *The War Amongst the Angels* (1996) as a sequel to *Blood*. Set in a future alternative Mississippi, the four central characters in *Blood* are experienced gamblers in the Game of Time or 'la zeitjuego'. These players can make decisions which affect their own destinies and the novel investigates this existential notion of having the freedom to choose your own future, and in doing so, affect the whole multiverse.

Equilibrium in a disordered world is achieved with pseudo-mathematics, through playing a type of virtual-reality game involving the symbiosis of player and character. The 'Chaos Engineers' are comic strip heroes from a typical 'space-opera' pulp magazine, although Moorcock never allows the reader to be completely certain of this, but the episodes with Captain Billy-Bob Begg and his corsairs fighting the evil 'Original Insect' soon become a post-modern pastiche of irony and self-reference where their adventures are woven into the main narrative. These 'jugadors' are able to 'fold' through time and space to the second ether to begin the true game, which is "a struggle between life and death." The game is psychic, involving the disembodied consciousness floating through ether, but only when spirit is combined with physical reality (blood) is fulfilment accomplished.

The ambiguous protagonist, the Rose, who is part flora, part human, first appeared in *The Revenge of the Rose* (1991) and is a character in Moorcock's dramatis personae with whom he has a particular empathy. She is not only a member of the ever-growing von Bek clan, but, we are told, is the author's own fictional cousin. In *Blood*, she alone seems to be enlightened enough to express a hope that, "The world is full of more wisdom than destructive ignorance ... Why can't that vast majority of us band together to achieve peace and equity?" This echoes Moorcock's anarchistic ideals of 'mutual aid'.

Once again Moorcock writes on a grand scale. *The War Amongst the Angels* culminates in Armageddon but Moorcock manages to provide metaphysics with little moralising. The familiar Moorcockian pantheon fights the final battle for the balance, echoing many of the finales of his sword and sorcery tales. This time, however, there is a difference. A casual footnote states that "The War in Heaven had long since ceased to be between God and the Devil. Now it was between a myriad different interests, each increasingly losing sight of its original goals in a series of pointlessly cynical alliances." Those interests are still represented by the dualism of chaos and order, except now the terms have been refined and informed by the author's reading of science's chaos theory so that chaos becomes 'plurality', and law is the 'singularity'.

Echoing Moorcock's epic scope, chaos theory views the world macrocosmically, rather than in the quantum terms of particles and quarks. Popular science writer James Gleick identified the importance of the following question for chaos theorists – "in a universe ruled by entropy, drawing inexorably toward greater and greater disorder, how does order arise?" This same question is one that has obsessed Moorcock for more than thirty years

When interviewed Moorcock is explicit about his references in *Blood*: "Chaos theory is a distinct help in that it provides a logic system, which means you can develop fiction more readily. The more tools you've got the more you can structure something. Chaos theory has helped me enormously with that." Chaos theory claims to see patterns emerge within scientific irregularities – or as Gleick expresses it, "Life sucks order from a sea of disorder."

In the near future of *Blood* the world has become unstable due to the natural entropic pull, causing ultra-reality to leak violently from the Biloxi Fault and time is now measured by "degrees of deliquescence." Entropy inevitably leads to a gradual dissipation into nothingness as a natural state but Moorcock's work also offers an alternative to entropy. Love and life-affirming sexuality can replace drained energy and allow individuals to rediscover or recreate their identities and empower them to travel the moonbeam paths of the multiverse to a new time or plane of existence.

Moorcock tackles metaphysical questions and the Rose states their true aim – "We're playing for the power to change the human condition." Moorcock's presentation of God is always as a benign and absent abstraction, or the closest he gets to identifying the creator is as 'the Great Mood'. He does however, use the scientific concept of fractals to explain how we are smaller versions of infinity or 'echoes of some lost original'.

It remains for us to entertain ourselves and play our hand with the greatest skill. Life is a gamble and a gambol, or a comic book, and the characters in 'The Second Ether' series are creating worlds as much as Moorcock himself. They appear to become the characters in the game they are playing, leaving the edges between play and reality blurred and ambivalent, creating a post-modern Moebius strip of never-ending layers. We are left frantically searching for meaning in our chaotic voyages across malleable landscapes, adrift in a steam boat or dirigible heading towards the 'Biloxi Fault' portending uncertainty.

Moorcock has also been enticed into returning to his comic book beginnings and from November 1997 DC published a successful 12 monthly comic series called *Michael Moorcock's Multiverse,* scripted by the author himself. The comic merges stories of the Rose, Elric and a reincarnation of Sexton Blake, Sir Seaton Begg, an eternal champion distantly related to von Bek. The story 'Moonbeams and Roses' recasts some of the characters from *Blood*.

The comics add further understanding to the concept of the Multiverse, which, we are told, is made up of "Countless versions of the old stories which we learn from our dreams, which are echoed by our own stories, which are, in turn, retold... and which we are sometimes able to change." The Rose is given great prominence, as she is in *The War Amongst the Angels*. She is the eternal champion – "I have one personality and a million selves" – and as such she is "sworn to bring coherence out of chaos and chaos out of stagnation."

Once again, in the comics, Moorcock raises and develops his favourite themes that enable us to dream of exotic adventures wherein that Romantic spirit of chaos eternally defeats the dull, predictable and soulless singularity of Reason.

The three stories are inter-linked and merge together in the final issue as Count Zodiac (an albino), Begg and a certain Jerry Cornelius unify into one champion whilst Elric confronts King Silverskin who is every aspect of the eternal champion. By absorbing Silverskin Elric creates "an unrepeatable moment of absolute harmony – a single chance of redemption for the entire multiverse." It is the Rose, however, who finally defeats the evil amalgamation of Prince Gaynor the Damned (who has previously confronted Corum and Elric) and Paul Minct (who appeared in *Blood*).

The comics are also a chance for Moorcock to make cross-references to earlier novels such as *The Brothel In Rosenstrasse*, to resurrect popular characters such as Moonglum, the eternal companion, and also to develop his own self-referencing. In 'Moonbeams and Roses' not only is Moorcock himself a player and observer at the Terminal Café, but he is joined by the artist, Walter Simonson.

Moorcock's collaboration with fellow fantasy writer Storm Constantine, *Silverheart* (2000), is subtitled 'A Novel of the Multiverse' and it introduces a new champion, Max Silverskin, whose surname links him with the *MMM* comics and with the new Elric novels.

When asked about the practicalities of co-writing a novel Moorcock is more than willing to give details. He explained his working relationship with Storm Constantine in the following way: "I was originally asked to provide a scenario for a [computer] game … Once we'd agreed the basic idea I sat down and began a scenario so detailed that it became a short novel of some 45,000 words … It's pretty much a good fifty-fifty collaboration, with Storm adding characteristic elements." She acknowledges Michael Moorcock as her main inspiration as an adolescent fantasy reader.

Its existence as a novel is not wholly satisfying as *Silverheart* suffers from the need for a trite quest and the unnecessary fighting so essential to the gaming format. The protagonist, Max Silverskin, searches for objects and travels through magical realms, making it a fascinating idea for the computer animator and game-player, but something of a clichéd novel.

Even if it is not written solely by Moorcock, *Silverheart* contains a multitude of Moorcockian signatures and devices. The introduction is written by 'Cornelius Begg', amalgamating two Moorcock characters, and the female protagonist is once again another incarnation of the Rose. The theme is strongly that of the balance of chaos and order, necessary to maintain the multiverse and the novel ends with Moorcock's traditional epiphany and reconciliation.

The novel introduces The Council of the Metal, which, with its unchanging orthodoxy and medieval feudal class system, runs the city of Karadur. Law and order is represented by Captain Coffin and his secret police and symbolised by the Gragonatt Fortress, from which Max Silverskin, thief and folk-hero, escapes by supernatural means. A mysterious voice challenges Max to "discover what you are or may be", which is surely a philosophical quest for each and every one of us.

Max discovers Karadur's parallel city, Shriltasi, a land of magic ('barishi') that was separated after the 'Reformation', which like our own Enlightenment in 18th century Europe, looked down on all that was not scientific and logical. Max's adventures begin to make more sense once he meets the Ashen folk and some of his own relatives, from whom he learns to control his own magical powers. He begins to question his own social programming and learn to feel beyond the limiting human senses. Rose discovers that "tradition is a blindfold" and Serenia Silverskin teaches her son Max that "Death is not a thing to be feared" and that the safest passage is "the middle path. Extremes of any kind are to be avoided."

Rose goes against her own father, Lord Iron, ruler of the Council of Metal, whose belief is that "Millennia have taught us never to change our customs." Max slowly comes to the realisation that "The Lords of the Metal didn't just control Karadur, they controlled reality. The powers of communication and authority were theirs. They wrote the history books, determining what was true and false. They castigated innovative thought, so that even the most intelligent citizens were almost incapable of thinking for themselves."

Lord Iron believes that Shriltasi is a place of evil, but the city Max discovers is merely different and he learns that magic can be used for the powers of good. His quest involves collecting the usual jewels, weapons and the other McGuffins of fantasy literature, and the novel is typical sword and sorcery in that respect, although Moorcock and Constantine avoid presenting evil stereotypes.

The setting of the novel is not specifically representative of our own world although there is reference to the Egyptian goddess of fire, Sekmet, who has the head of a lioness and is linked with war and the sun. We are merely told that Karadur-Shriltasi is "the core of the multiverse, that the fate of the city determines the nature of all ordered matter in myriad worlds and countless realities." Humans, it seems are the guardians of the multiverse, despite their many weaknesses and limitations. The weakness that particularly distinguishes humans is their natural prejudice and hostility to things and people who are different. Rose experiences a moment of enlightenment in which she sees the multiverse and her own relationship to it – "all things were upon the web and if one strand vibrated, all others must feel it." This is a valuable lesson – that actions do have consequences and effects on others.

Silverheart is an easy and exciting read, full of gothic textures. It also contains a simple yet important message for its readers. As Max's own mother warns, "It is a mistake to think that mundane reality is the only one." It is for this very reason that everyone should read fantasy literature to learn about the different truths and realities. Fantasy teaches us to dream, expand our own knowledge and experience, to learn to escape and look beyond our own limitations.

Coda

Moorcock is both avant-garde and popular, translated into many languages, yet his novels rarely reach the best-seller lists or university reading lists in Britain. It can be argued that he is ahead of his time or too experimental for the general public, but another reason for his marginalisation could have something to do with the suspicion still felt towards fantasy. This ignorance reveals a fallacy and problem with our culture's reception of literature. There is also the problem of trying to pigeon-hole Moorcock's works. Although he is usually referred to as a science fiction writer by lazy booksellers and critics he is not embraced by all science fiction or even all fantasy readers. This suits him well as Moorcock would rather be remembered as a popular author who broke the boundaries of the conventional genres. The difficulty is that he falls between fantasy and mainstream literature, which causes problems for the critics.

Fantasy is an undervalued literary impulse. Since the Enlightenment, western culture has placed more value on rational thinking and demanded a more exact form of naturalistic representation in its artistic expressions. Since then symbolism and myth have been regarded with some suspicion and, today, fantasy suffers from the same prejudice. It is important to remember that realism, like fantasy, is only another literary convention that has its own limitations as reality itself cannot be confined to materialistic description because it is full of ambiguity, dreams, paradox, symbol and mystery. Fantasy literature is surely a more accurate, if not satisfactory, form for expressing the complex reality of our own strange lives.

Fantasy has something important to offer in terms of re-evaluating our cultural heritage and offering insight into a more mystical and spiritual reality. Moorcock, as a writer, explores themes and subjects that others dare not confront. He is also an elusive and protean writer whose works blur the generic boundaries and he is doing as much as anyone to bring fantasy into the literary mainstream.

What makes Moorcock's work stand above that of others, is that whilst some writers choose to present us with a microcosm of reality, Moorcock prefers the larger canvas of eternal time and space: not just this universe but the infinite continuum of the entire multiverse. Each myth he conjures challenges us in our own private struggles with chaos and order:

"I do celebrate the mythologising creativity of the human mind ... As ecstatic dimension upon dimension unfolded, scattered, blended and bent, making every object a thing of intense beauty, sometimes of terror; as extraordinary encrusted patterns revealed themselves in the most familiar things, I was consumed with the most profound emotion at the harmony I sensed in the whole unseen multiverse."

Michael Moorcock 1998.

Selected Bibliography

For a more complete bibliography please see John Davey's *Michael Moorcock: A Reader's Guide* (Jayde Design – available from The Nomads of the Time Streams). This excellent guide not only lists British first editions and revisions, but also comments on how the books are categorised and sequenced. John Davey's notes and comments are extremely helpful to all readers and this remains the definitive bibliography, approved by Moorcock himself.

There follows here a list of Michael Moorcock's novels, short story collections, non-fiction and graphic novels, although trying to bring order to the chaos is a complicated procedure as Moorcock has produced something close to a hundred books. I have also added some websites and other areas of related interest.

My bibliography begins with the republished Millenium/Orion editions, which are still available in good bookshops. However, not all of Moorcock's books are still in print and sometimes titles have been changed. Many short stories have been collected in different anthologies a number of times.

Beginning in 1992, the British publishers, Millennium/Orion reissued practically all the titles that fit into his 'Eternal Champion Multiverse' in fourteen weighty volumes, of which the largest exceeds

800 pages. This was done with the help of John Davey. I have tried to include the date of the first edition and where necessary added a short descriptive comment, which may help to show the various connections.

The series attempts to create a uniform omnibus collection of these particular books and involves some revision. Moorcock is not frightened of tampering with earlier work so as to develop a clearer interconnectedness.

Most of the amendments are slight, involving names, so that familiar characters can be reincarnated to make interconnections more explicit. For example, an early story from *New Worlds* 154, 'The Pleasure Garden of Felipe Sagittarius' has been adapted to fit in with *The War Hound and the World's Pain*, and the narrator's name is changed to von Bek, accordingly. The same is done to the story 'Flux' in Sailing to Utopia. Moorcock also extensively expanded the last two chapters of *The Steel Tsar*, the third book in 'A Nomad of the Time Streams', chronicling the adventures of Oswald Bastable. The rewriting allows Moorcock to change a few names, and bring in references to books he wrote in the nineties. The new chapters are full of commentary regarding time and the multiverse, developing some of Moorcock's political interest in anarchism.

Jeff Gardiner

The Tale of the Eternal Champion
Millennium/Orion Omnibus Editions.

Volume 1 – **VON BEK** (1992)
The War Hound and the World's Pain (1981) Gothic romance.
The City in the Autumn Stars (1986) A sequel set in the age of enlightenment.
'The Pleasure Garden of Felipe Sagittarius'(1965). A revised but key story.

Volume 2 – **THE ETERNAL CHAMPION** (1992)
The Eternal Champion (1970: novella 1962) Erekosë.
Phoenix In Obsidian (1970) Urlik Skarsol.
The Dragon In the Sword (1986) John Daker.

Volume 3 – **HAWKMOON** (1992)
The Jewel In the Skull (1967)
The Mad God's Amulet (1968)
The Sword Of the Dawn (1968)
The Runestaff (1969)

Volume 4 – **CORUM** (1992)
The Knight of the Swords (1971)
The Queen of the Swords (1971)
The King of the Swords (1971)

Volume 5 – **SAILING TO UTOPIA** (1993)
The Ice Schooner (1969) Based loosely on Conrad's *The Rescue*.
The Black Corridor (1969) Sf – co-written with Hilary Bailey.
The Distant Suns (1975) Jerry Cornelius tale c/w with James Cawthorn.
'Flux' (1963) A story co-written with Barrington Bayley.

Volume 6 – **A NOMAD OF THE TIME STREAMS** (1993)
The Warlord of the Air (1971)
The Land Leviathan (1974)
The Steel Tsar (1981)

Volume 7 – **THE DANCERS AT THE END OF TIME** (1993)
An Alien Heat (1972)
The Hollow Lands (1974)
The End of All Songs (1976)

Volume 8 – **ELRIC OF MELNIBONÉ** (1993)
Elric of Melniboné (1972)
The Fortress of the Pearl (1989)
The Sailor on the Seas of Fate (1976)
The Weird of the White Wolf (1977) including 'The Dreaming City' (1961) but excluding 'The Dream of Earl Aubec', which is in volume 13 – *Earl Aubec*.
Many of the Elric stories have been previously published and anthologised.

Volume 9 – **THE NEW NATURE OF THE CATASTROPHE** (1993)
An anthology of over 30 Jerry Cornelius stories by Moorcock and others, including the famous IT cartoon strip (1971) and much of the original artwork. Originally released as *The Nature of the Catastrophe* (1971), this edition includes new stories and incorporates material from *The Lives and Times of Jerry Cornelius* (1976).

Volume 10 – **THE PRINCE WITH THE SILVER HAND** (1993)
(Sequel to *Corum*)
The Bull and the Spear (1973)
The Oak and the Ram (1973)
The Sword and the Stallion (1974)

Volume 11 – **LEGENDS FROM THE END OF TIME** (1993)
Legends from the End of Time (1976)
The Transformation of Miss Mavis Ming (1977) This was retitled *Constant Fire* but, mistakenly, only the last chapter was printed so they replaced the entire novella within *Behold The Man and Other Stories*.
Elric At the End of Time (1981) Originally illustrated by Rodney Matthews.

Volume 12 – **STORMBRINGER** (1993)
(Continuing the Elric series)
The Sleeping Sorceress (1971)
The Revenge of the Rose (1991)
The Bane of the Black Sword (1977) Including stories written between 1967–77 but excluding 'To Rescue Tanelorn', which is in *Earl Aubec*.
Stormbringer (1965)

Volume 13 – **EARL AUBEC and Other Stories** (1993)
The Golden Barge (1979) His first novel completed in 1957.
32 short stories, most of them previously published in *My Experiences in the Third World War, The Opium General, The Time Dweller, Moorcock's Book of Martyrs, Casablanca* et al., including 'The Deep Fix' (1963). This volume also includes previously uncollected stories.

Volume 14 – **COUNT BRASS** (1993) The end of the Eternal Champion cycle.
(Sequel to *Hawkmoon*)
Count Brass (1973).
The Champion of Garathorm (1973) The Eternal Champion becomes Queen Ilian.
The Quest for Tanelorn (1975) Four champions unite to attain Cosmic Balance.

Phoenix House Omnibus editions

THE CORNELIUS QUARTET (Phoenix/Orion 1993)
(The Jerry Cornelius tetralogy)
The Final Programme (1968)
A Cure For Cancer (1971)
The English Assassin (1972)
The Condition of Muzak (1977)

A CORNELIUS CALENDAR (Phoenix 1993)
The Adventures of Una Persson and Catherine Cornelius in the Twentieth Century (1976)
The Entropy Tango (1981) Tie-in with an unreleased Deep Fix album.
Gold Diggers of 1977 (1980) aka *The Great Rock'n'Roll Swindle* – film tie-in.
The Alchemist's Question (1984) published in *The Opium General*.

BEHOLD THE MAN AND OTHER STORIES (Phoenix 1994)
Behold the Man (1969) Karl Glogauer becomes Jesus.
Constant Fire (1977) See *Legends From the End of Time*.
Breakfast In the Ruins (1972) Episodic 'sequel' to *Behold the Man*.

Other Novels and Collections

Sojan (Savoy 1977) Contains short stories from 1957–75 and some non-fiction.
The Sundered Worlds (Compact 1965) aka *The Blood Red Game*.
Kane of Old Mars (originally Compact 1965) aka *Warrior of Mars*.
The Fireclown (Compact 1965) aka *The Winds of Limbo*.
The Twilight Man (Compact 1966) aka *The Shores of Death*.
Somewhere In The Night (Compact 1966) revised as *The Chinese Agent*.
The Printer's Devil (Compact 1966) revised as *The Russian Intelligence*.
The Wrecks of Time (Ace 1967) aka *The Rituals of Infinity* (Arrow 1971).
Gloriana; or, The Unfulfill'd Queen (Allison and Busby 1978: revised Phoenix 1993)

Col. Pyat - Between the Wars
Byzantium Endures (Secker and Warburg 1981)
The Laughter of Carthage (Secker and Warburg 1984)
Jerusalem Commands (Jonathan Cape 1992)
Vengeance of Rome (in preparation)

The Brothel in Rosenstrasse (NEL 1982) A novel about another von Bek.
Mother London (Secker and Warburg 1988)

The Second Ether (Orion)
Blood (1994)
Fabulous Harbours (1995)
The War Amongst the Angels (1996)

Tales From the Texas Woods (Mojo 1997) Anthology of new stories and non-fiction.
The King of the City (Scribner 2000) Nominally a sequel to *Mother London*.
Silverheart (Earthlight 2000) A collaboration with Storm Constantine.
London Bone (Scribner 2001) A collection of previously published stories.

An Elric Trilogy
The Dreamthief's Daughter (Earthlight 2001) The return of Elric.
The Skrayling Tree (Earthlight 2002)
The Swordsman of Mirenburg (in preparation)

Firing the Cathedral (PS Publishing 2002) A Jerry Cornelius novella.

Non-Fiction

The Retreat From Liberty (Zomba Books 1983) Anarchistic polemic.
Letters From Hollywood (Harrap 1986) Travelog/autobiog with art by
Michael Foreman.
Wizardry and Wild Romance (V. Gollancz 1987) Study of Fantasy literature.
Fantasy: The 100 Best Books (Xanadu 1988) with James Cawthorn.
Death Is No Obstacle (Savoy 1992) Interviews with Colin Greenland.

Illustrated Novella / Portfolio

Elric: The Return to Melnibone (Jayde Design 1997) illustrated by Philippe
Druillet.

As Editor

Tarzan Adventures (1957–58)
Sexton Blake Library (1959–61)
New Worlds #142–207 (1964–1973) and #212–216 (1978–79) & #221 (1996)
SF Reprise (1966–67)

Music

Deep Fix:
   New World's Fair (UAG 1975: Griffen CD 1995)
   Brothel In Rosenstrasse (Cyborg 1992)
Hawkwind:
   Warrior On the Edge of Time (UAG 1975)
   Sonic Attack (RCA 1981)
   Zones (Flicknife 1983)
   Live Chronicles (Griffen 1994)
Also worked with Robert Calvert, Nik Turner and wrote songs for Blue
Oyster Cult.

Comics

Michael Moorcock's Multiverse (DC 1998) comics #1–12.

Film

The Land that Time Forgot, c/w James Cawthorn, based on E R Burroughs'
novel.

Graphic Novels (adaptations of Moorcock's work)

The Swords of Heaven, The Flowers of Hell (Simon and Schuster 1979) with Howard Chaykin.
The Jewel In the Skull (Savoy) James Cawthorn.
The Crystal and the Amulet (Savoy 1986) James Cawthorn.
Stormbringer (Savoy) James Cawthorn.
Elric of Melniboné (First USA 1987) Roy Thomas & P Craig Russell.
Elric: Sailor on the Seas of Fate (First USA 1987) Thomas, Gilbert and Freeman.
Stormbringer (Dark Horse/Topps 2001) P Craig Russell.

The Time Centre Times is produced by The Nomads of the Time Streams: the International Michael Moorcock Appreciation Society, and is edited by Ian Covell, John and Maureen Davey and D J Rowe.
For more details about The Nomads of the Time Streams please contact D J Rowe at: 'Mo Dhachaidh', LochAwe Village, LochAwe-by-Dalmally, Argyll PA33 1AQ, Scotland.

Selected Websites Relating to Michael Moorcock

www.multiverse.org – The Official Moorcock Site/Nomads of the Time Streams.
www.moorcock.cjb.net – The Terminal Café – Moorcock Information Node.
www.eclipse.co.uk/sweetdespise/moorcock – Cartographer of the Multiverse.
www.newworldsmagazine.com
www.stormbringer.net – The Eternal Champion & Elric.
www.hawkwind.com – Official Hawkwind homepage.
www.thing.de/projekte/future/moorcock.htm – Robert Calvert homepage.
www.revolutionsf.com
www.sfsite.com – fantastic metropolis.

Reference and Books of Related Interest

Aldiss, Brian *The Trillion Year Spree*, Victor Gollancz 1986
Armitt, Lucie *Theorising the Fantastic*, Hodder 1996
Arnheim, Rudolf *Entropy and Art: An essay on disorder and order*, California 1971
Ballard, J.G. *A User's Guide to the Millennium*, Flamingo 1997
Bradbury, Malcolm *The Modern British Novel*, Penguin 1993
Burns & Sugnet *The Imagination On Trial*, Allison & Busby 1981
Camp, L Sprague de *Literary Swordsmen and Sorcerers*, Wisconsin 1976
Carter, Lin *Imaginary Worlds: The Art of Fantasy*, N.Y. 1973
Clute, John *Science Fiction: The Illustrated Encyclopedia*, Dorling Kindersley 1995
Clute, J & John Grant *The Encyclopedia of Fantasy*, Orbit 1997
Greenland, Colin *The Entropy Exhibition*, Routledge, Kegan & Paul 1983
Hume, Kathryn *Fantasy and Mimesis*, Methuen 1984
Jackson, Rosemary *Fantasy: A Literature of Subversion*, Routledge 1981
James, Edward *Science Fiction in the Twentieth Century*, Oxford 1994
Jung, C.G. *Modern Man In Search of a Soul*, Routledge 1933
Kropotkin, Peter *The Conquest of Bread and Other Writing*, Cambridge 1995
Malmgren, Carl *Worlds Apart*, Indiana 1991
Melly, George *Revolt Into Style*, Oxford 1970
Nicholls, Peter *The Encyclopedia Of Science Fiction*, Granada 1981
Nicholls, Stan *Wordsmiths of Wonder*, Orbit 1993
Nuttall, Jeff *Bomb Culture*, MacGibbon & Kee 1968
Parrinder, Patrick *Shadows of the Future*, Liverpool 1995
Platt, Charles *Dream Makers*, Xanadu, London 1980
Rabkin & Slusser (Ed) *Styles of Creation*, Georgia 1992
Scholes, Robert *Fabulation and Metafiction*, Illinois 1979
Scholes, R.& E Rabkin *Science Fiction*, Oxford 1977
Schweitzer, D. (Ed) *Exploring Fantasy Worlds*, Borgo Press, California 1985
Seed, David (Ed) *Anticipations*, Liverpool 1995
Slusser, G & T Shippey *Fiction 2000*, U.S. 1992
Tawn, Brian *Dude's Dreams; the Music of Michael Moorcock*, Hawkfan publications, 1997

The Spiral Garden

The acclaimed fantasy collection by Louise Cooper

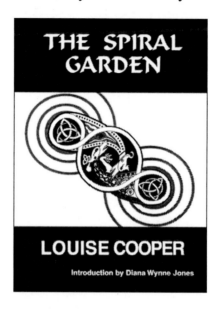

Louise Cooper has delighted fantasy readers of all ages since 1973 with over 50 novels to her credit. *The Spiral Garden* collects five of her finer short stories, including the brand new tale 'St Gumper's Feast'.

With an introduction by Diana Wynne Jones

Signed (by Louise Cooper, Diana Wynne Jones and artist Cas Sandall) and Numbered 200 copy limited edition.
110 page A5 paperback

Only £5.99

Send a cheque or postal order for £5.99 (plus 50p p&p UK) to BFS Publications, c/o 3 Tamworth Close, Lower Earley, Berks, RG6 4EQ. Or order online by credit card at www.britishfantasysociety.org.uk.

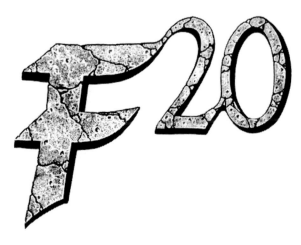

T W O

Edited by David J Howe, M P N Sims and L H Maynard

Seven deadly sins … seven stunning authors.
All-new fiction from:

**STORM CONSTANTINE, JULIET E. MCKENNA,
JANE WELCH, FREDA WARRINGTON, LOUISE COOPER,
JUSTINA ROBSON** and **SUZANNE J BARBIERI.**

Illustrated by Bob Covington, David Bezzina, Carolyn Edwards,
Lara Bandilla and Alf Klosterman.

"a rich feast of fantasy … an impressive collection,
highly recommended" *Vector*

Signed and Numbered limited edition.
120 page A5 perfect bound chap-book

Only £7.99

Send a cheque or postal order for £7.99 (plus 50p p&p UK) to BFS
Publications, c/o 3 Tamworth Close, Lower Earley, Berks, RG6 4EQ.
Or order online by credit card at www.britishfantasysociety.org.uk.

OTHER PUBLICATIONS FROM

SHOCKS
by Ronald Chetwynd-Hayes.
A collection of four spine-chilling stories from Britain's
Prince of Chill. **£6.00** (60pp A5 chapbook).

MISCELLANY MACABRE
by Ken Cowley.
Step into the world of Ken Cowley, a world peopled with ghosts,
phantoms and horrors from ages past. Hear Count Dracula's story in
his own words, learn the secret of a dark and skeletal night-time
visitor, discover a shop which deals in memories ... all these and more
can be found within. Introduction by Ramsey Campbell.
£5.99 (80pp A5 paperback).
SIGNED AND NUMBERED LIMITED EDITION

F^{20} Issue 1
Edited by M P N Sims, L H Maynard
and David J Howe.
Terrifying new stories of fantasy and horror from Derek M Fox,
Steve Savile, Paul Finch, Steve Lockley & Paul Lewis
and Tim Lebbon.
"A powerhouse collection of unputdownable horror and fantasy fiction"
Terror Tales Online
£6.99 (120pp A5 paperback book).
SIGNED AND NUMBERED LIMITED EDITION

*To order please add 50 pence postage and packing per item, and send
a cheque or postal order for the total amount (overseas orders please
write for further details) to:* **BFS Publications, c/o 3 Tamworth
Close, Lower Earley, Reading, Berks, RG6 4EQ**
Or order online by credit card from our secure store at:
www.britishfantasysociety.com